FRONTIER BOY

A Story of Oregon

FRONTIER BOY
A Story of Oregon
by Herbert E. Arntson

Illustrated by William Ferguson

IVES WASHBURN, INC.
NEW YORK

FRONTIER BOY
A Story of Oregon

LIBRARY OF CONGRESS CATALOG CARD NUMBER: 67-13346

MANUFACTURED IN THE UNITED STATES OF AMERICA

To
John Oak
and
Mary Turner

Contents

FRONTIER BOY
A Story of Oregon

Chapter 1

The Mountain Lion

DAVID'S HEART thumped as he moved quietly across the dark room of the cabin, and he listened for the sound to come again. It had been a frightening sound. He wasn't sure what it was, but it had awakened him suddenly.

His mother's voice came to him out of the shadows: "What was it, David?"

He went over to the one window, rested his hand on the sill, and stared out into the night. "I don't know," he said. "It was an animal. It must have been. A bear, maybe. Or—a mountain lion."

He heard her draw in her breath sharply. He knew what she was thinking about. Rosy and Betsy, in the barn.

He peered at the darkness. A faint, eerie glow of moonlight fell on the vague patch of ground nearby and edged

1

the looming shapes of trees farther back. Nothing moved out there. Nothing in the cold night stirred or made a sound.

Just the two of them were on the place now. His father, Jed, had left for The Dalles two days ago. There was not a soul within a mile of the farm. Unless Indians were prowling the woods. And that might be, for Oregon was a wild, lonely country in this year of 1849.

"David—"

The sound came again, without any warning. A snarl. A heavy snarl that ended in a throaty rattle. Just outside the door, under the dogtrot, between the cabin and the barn. Just a few feet away.

"What are we going to do, boy?"

He wiped his hands on his nightshirt. The cow and the horse were in danger. There was a gun in the corner of the room, by the door, and he knew what his father would do if he were here. Jed would load the gun. He would open the door and walk out there, in the night.

David hesitated. Perhaps if he didn't make any noise the animal would sniff around the barn, find that Rosy and Betsy were securely locked in, and then quietly sneak away into the woods. He thought of how it would be if he stepped outside, the gun in his hand—and a tawny shape came slinking toward him, creeping up behind him stealthily. Even though he was thirteen years old, he didn't feel that brave. And yet he knew he should go out there. They depended on Rosy for milk. And without Betsy, the horse—

There was a loud scratch of claws, a crack of wood, a splintering sound. A pause, and then a frightened whinny.

"David!"

He went quickly to the corner of the room, caught up the gun. He fumbled with the powder horn, got the cap off and shook powder into his palm, poured it down the barrel of the gun, his hands trembling. He wrapped a bullet in a cloth patch, shoved it down with the long ramrod.

There was another snarl, a rasping catlike noise, and he forced himself to put the cap back on the horn, hang it around his neck, and feel the percussion cap with his finger to make sure it was in place.

It was more terrifying now to think that perhaps he was too late. He slid the bar back from the door, lifted the latch, and pushed the door open a little. He raised the gun and pulled the hammer until it clicked loudly.

He stared into the night. Moonlight cut under the roof of the dogtrot, glowed across the chopping block, the handle of the ax, the pile of wood, and over the end of the barn. He swung the door wider, and the hinges creaked. He saw black shadows, vague shapes, and he lifted the gun halfway to his shoulder.

Maybe it had gone. There was a thump of hooves on the hard dirt floor of the barn, the sound of the horse blowing loudly through her lips. He could tell that Betsy was frightened. He moved through the doorway, went down the one hewn step, and stood there for a moment looking from one side to the other, pointing the gun as he turned his head.

Slowly he went ahead, watching every scrap of a shadow, all the way to the barn door. He stared at it. He could just see that a board had been ripped away. He thought he saw three long streaks across the wood, like the marks of claws. He was sure he knew what had done that. He was sure it was a mountain lion.

3

And where was it now? In the barn, lurking there and looking out at him? He stood still, listened to the noises that Betsy made. It sounded like she was thrashing back and forth, bumping into things.

He was barely conscious of the first sound as the lion leaped out through the broken door. The feet padded twice on the earth, there was a piercing cry—and the shadow hurtled toward him.

He acted in the same instant. He lifted the gun, pulled the trigger. There was a roar and a stab of red flame, and a shape that brushed past him.

He crowded against the barn, took hold of the gun by the barrel, to use it as a club. The animal sprawled heavily on the ground, rolled into the open, and jerked wildly. For a moment it looked as though it would scramble onto its feet. Its head lifted, there was a flash of eyes and teeth, a hiss of breath. Slowly it crumpled, its legs twitching.

A light gleamed in the cabin door. He looked up to see his mother standing there, a candle in her left hand. Something glinted in her right hand. The carving knife. She was holding it like a dagger.

"What is it, boy?"

He tried to speak, found his mouth was too dry. He swallowed.

"A mountain lion. It was in the barn. It jumped out through that broken board."

"In the barn! What about the animals?"

His shadow danced eerily on the end of the barn as they walked toward it. He opened the door and his mother held the light so it shone inside.

The cow turned her head toward them and looked at them steadily, her eyes wide and her jaws champing. They looked at the horse. She was pressed against the far

4

wall, her sides rising and falling swiftly, her breath coming in gasps. She was trembling. And across the side of her neck, spreading down her forequarters, was a glistening red stain.

"Davy—she's been hurt!"

David went to her, caught her by the bridle and patted her muzzle. She tried to jerk free, but he hung on tight. "Easy, girl, easy now—don't be afraid, Betsy!" He looked at her wound while his mother brought the light closer. It was an ugly gash.

"Poor Betsy! Here, boy, hold this candle. I'm going in the cabin and get something to put on that." His mother hurried out of the barn, and David held the light up so she could see. He rubbed his head against the side of the horse's nose.

"I'm sorry, Betsy," he whispered. "I'm sorry I didn't come out right away. It was my fault."

When Mrs. Carder returned in a few minutes, she brought a handful of clean rags, a kettle of hot water, and a small jar.

"Davy, set that candle somewhere safe and help me, boy."

He wedged it in the wide crack of a wooden block, and as the light flickered and waved, his mother handed him a rag soaked in water. Gently he began to wash around Betsy's wound, patting her and talking as he did so. He didn't dare get close to the raw edges of the gash.

"David, you hold her muzzle while I see if I can just dab that a little cleaner, and spread some of this pitch over that. Easy, Betsy—we're trying to help you, girl. Gently, now."

David hung on tightly while his mother very carefully smoothed the pitch in place. The horse tried to shy away

5

and bumped against the wall but Mrs. Carder kept working steadily until the cut was covered.

"There, now. That's as much as we can do." She picked up the candle and the kettle, and gazed at David. "At least it will stay clean that way. It should heal before long. She'll be all right. It was a courageous thing you did, boy. Mighty dangerous, too. I'm glad that all we have to worry about is that scratch on Betsy. It makes me weak thinking what could have happened. Bring the jar with you when you come. I'm going back to the cabin."

She walked out of the barn, paused by the dead animal for a moment, and went on into the cabin. David stepped outside, shut the barn door, and pulled a board across the opening before he fastened the door. There was enough moonlight now to see the mountain lion, and he stood beside it a long time.

He remembered what his father had said to him when he left only a few days ago. He remembered every word: "Son, there are some things a man does whether he wants to or not. It's like that now. I want to stay here and take care of you and your mother, and tend to the place. I have to build that fence and get the garden ready. Pretty soon I must plow the field, and sow the wheat. But you know, son—there are families, just like ours, that need help getting down the river from The Dalles. It's up to me to do what I can to help. And I won't worry about you two. I know I can depend on you to take care of the place until I get back."

David thought about Betsy again, and the ugly wound. It wouldn't have happened if he had frightened the animal away as soon as he heard it. It wouldn't have happened if he had not been afraid.

6

The next morning was blustery and cold, and the February wind swept through the trees around the cabin, tossing them like great feathers, flailing the branches of the alders like skinny brooms in the air, and whistling through the dark firs. David put Rosy out in the patch that was her pasture, the place they would turn into a garden when it was time, and when he had built a fence around it. He went back to look at Betsy. She was calm now, and she nickered at him as he came close. He could see that the scratch was not as long as he had thought, and the pitch covered it well. He tied a rope to her bridle and led her out, staying away from the tawny shape that still lay there.

"Easy girl, easy now," he said, and stopped to rub the white spot between her eyes. She nuzzled against his shoulder, and he took her along slowly, over to a place where she could browse, and there tied the rope with plenty of slack. It had not been a hard winter, and there was still enough grass for her.

Then he inspected the mountain lion. He prodded it with his foot. It didn't look so big in the daylight, and he wondered that it had been strong enough to break into the barn. His mother came to the door and looked out.

"What are you going to do with it, son?"

"I'll skin it," he said. "Skin it and peg the hide on the outside of the barn. Just like Dad did with the deer."

"And rub it in well with salt. You know about that."

"I'll do a good job, Mom."

He got a length of rope and his hunting knife, tugged and hauled the carcass until it was well away from the cabin, down in the woods near the trail that led to the Griffins' place. There he tossed an end of the rope over a

7

branch, pulled until the animal was up where he could work on it. It wasn't a neat job at all, but finally he was finished, and he brought the soft hide back to the barn, whittled little alder pegs, stretched the skin as tight as he could, nailing it to the side of the building with the pegs. After that he scraped it with a stiff scrap of cedar, and rubbed handfuls of salt all over it to preserve it. When he was through, he stepped back to study it.

It was a fair pelt. If it turned out all right, he could make a coat of it, perhaps a coat that would disguise him so well he could even sneak up on the old beaver that had a dam down on Scat Creek. It would be a fine hunting coat. It would be much nicer than the overcoat he had been wearing—an old blanket with a hole cut in the middle for his head to stick through.

Several days passed before the hide was ready to use. He had worked on it every day, rubbing and scraping it. Still, it became stiff as a board, and no matter how much he rubbed it, it did not become soft and pliable.

Somehow they managed to make a coat out of it. True enough, there wasn't quite enough to go around him, and Mrs. Carder cut up the old overcoat blanket and stitched it in place for the front and the sleeves, and had enough left for a fur cap. They left one paw hanging at the side of the coat, claws and all.

When he tried it on and set the new cap on his head, his mother put down her heavy needle and rested her hands on the table.

It didn't bend very easily. It felt like a suit of armor. But it was a coat, a real hunter's coat, and he was proud of it.

"How does it look, Mom?"

8

"Well—it makes you look like a real mountain man. Maybe after awhile, when you've used it more, some of the stiffness will wear out of it. One thing's for sure—it will keep the cold off your shoulders. The wind will never blow through it."

She walked to the window and looked out. "I've been thinking, son, that maybe you'd like to go on a little trip. Now that you have a new coat this might be just the right time. We need flour and bacon. There is enough wheat left, and dried peas, and even a little coffee. But I'm getting tired of trying to cook without flour. You could ride Betsy. She's all right now. Nothing left but a scar."

David nodded slowly. He had seen the scar, the three straight marks side by side. The scar would always be there.

She turned toward him. "You think you could ride her to Oregon City? In your new coat? Maybe Betsy won't let you get near her in that outfit. Or maybe you want me to go. She can't carry both of us, you know."

David watched her as she walked to the fireplace and put another stick of wood on the fire. He had been to Oregon City with Jed. He knew the trail, where to cross the river, how to find Mr. Dickins' place. He had never gone there alone. For just an instant he wondered if his mother had another reason for asking him to go. As though he should do something by himself, to prove that he could.

"I'll go, Mom. I'll leave early in the morning."

"All right, son." She touched his shoulder. "You take the gun with you. Go straight to Mr. Dickins' store and tell him your father will pay for the things when he comes back. Be sure you keep everything covered and dry, and tied carefully. I'll put up a lunch for you."

9

And so it was that the next morning, in a cold and wet drizzly dawn, he brought Betsy out of the barn, put her blanket and rawhide saddle in place. She shied away from his new coat, but he patted her and talked to her until she quieted down. Mrs. Carder came out with his lunch tied in a cloth, and handed it to him with a scrap of old newspaper on which she had written her list. He swung into the saddle, and she handed him the lunch and the list. And the gun.

"Do you want to keep the gun here, Mom?"

She shook her head. "If I have trouble I can lock the door of the cabin. Or I can run for help to the Griffins. Or Mr. Martin. You take it, Davy. I'd feel better if you did." She gave him the powder horn, the pouch with the bullets and caps, and the corkscrew worm to clean the gun. He hung them over his shoulder and laid the gun across his knees. "Now you have all the things you need—you know where to go, and what to say to Mr. Dickins."

"Yes, Mom. And I'll be back tonight. If anything happens, I'll be here tomorrow. But nothing will happen. Don't you worry."

She reached up and patted his hand. "There's nothing for me to worry about. I know you'll manage beautifully. I have confidence in you. Just you remember that, son. And be careful. You hear, now?"

He nodded his head, clucked his tongue, flapped the reins, and Betsy moved away from the cabin. At the edge of the field, where the narrow path wound through the trees, David turned, saw his mother standing in the dog-trot, waving her apron at him. He waved back just as Betsy jogged behind the trunk of a great fir, and then he could no longer see his mother, or the cabin, or even the little field beside it.

It was darker here where the trail curved around clumps of vine maple, around trees, by the old stump that stuck up in the way like a huge gray tooth. And it would have been quieter here except that dry sticks crackled under Betsy's hooves and low limbs brushed noisily against him. Whenever he had to crowd past an overhanging clump of branches or brush, he was sure to be showered with water.

He didn't mind at all. It was a fine thing to be riding high in the saddle, watching Betsy's head bob, holding the reins with just the right slack and letting the woods slip by him. It was a good feeling to be off alone with his gun and his gear. No one else in the world was responsible for what he was doing. No one but himself. He pressed his shoulders against his hard coat and prodded Betsy with his heels.

"Giddap, Betsy," he said. "We don't have any time to waste," and she broke into a smart trot.

Through the woods they went, past the narrow places where branches would have to be trimmed, across open spots where the rain made the grass and dirt soft, on down the slope beyond, where the ruts led past the Griffins' field. He saw smoke coming out of the Griffin cabin on the side of the far hill, and thought that perhaps he saw somebody walking from the house to the barn. He flipped the reins and looked straight ahead. He was not anxious to visit with Dan, or Mr. Griffin. Dan was a little older and taller, and he was likely to be sullen. David had never been able to get along with him very well.

Up the slope he went, over the low crest where he could see the long stretches below, and then he settled down for the miles that followed. Now and then he stopped to rest Betsy, or adjust the saddle, or just to look

11

around him. The rawhide saddle squeaked and the wooden stirrups were clumsy, and that was the way they should be. Things that were meant to be strong enough for a man to use were always rough and awkward.

A little before noon he came to the shore of the Willamette River. The old man who ran the ferry was waiting there, sitting under a tree and smoking. When David rode up, he came forward, knocking the ashes out of his pipe. This morning, he said, he wouldn't collect anything for the trip across the river. David could pay him in gunpowder on his way back. So Betsy was urged up the planks onto the barge, tied to a post, and the slow trip across the river began.

The man stood in the front of the barge, pushing two great oars back and forth, while David helped to pole them away from the shore. The water was quieter at this point and David was surprised they drifted so slowly downstream. The current ran more swiftly in the middle of the river, as he could tell by watching the trees on the shore, but a little sand bar formed a place they could pull into before they had gone too far. Here they came to shore at a low bank, the ferry was made snug to a stump, and David led Betsy onto land, climbed into the saddle, and rode on toward Oregon City.

Oregon City was a very odd town. David wondered how it could hang on the side of the steep hill without slipping into the river below. There were several buildings, and a mill on an island. But the sight that impressed David the most was, of course, the great falls just above where the water cascaded and tumbled noisily, filling the air with its constant rushing sound.

As he jogged along the narrow, curving road, toward Mr. Dickins' store, he noticed that there were very few people. It had been a busy place. Now there were only a few men in sight, except for a dozen or so natives who walked slowly at the edge of the way, blankets draped over their shoulders. It was almost as though the town had been abandoned.

He remembered, as he came to the store. The men had gone to California, to mine for gold. He had heard his parents talk about it, how it had been like a fever that made men leave their jobs and their farms suddenly, and ride off toward Sacramento.

Mr. Dickins did not recognize David at first, and he blinked at him over his glasses while David stood in the middle of the store, his gun in one hand.

"I'm Jed's boy," he said.

The man slapped a hand on the counter. "Well! I should say you are. I can see that now. But a lot more boy than I saw the last time." He came around a pile of boxes and shook David's hand and thumped him on the shoulder. "There must be something in this country that turns children into men faster. You suppose it's all this rain?"

He laughed to himself as he went back behind his counter and leaned forward. "Now you want supplies. Is that right? Did you bring a list?"

David got out the scrap of paper and read from it while Mr. Dickins put things in a heap on the counter. When they were finished, the man rolled them in a piece of canvas and tied them into a clumsy bundle.

"You ought to be proud of your father, David, and I expect you are. Practically every man around here has left for the goldfields. Most of them don't seem to care what happens to the rest of us, or their farms, or anything else. But not Jed. No, sir. He could have gone. And probably he wanted to. But he knew those people needed help getting

13

down river with their animals and their supplies. They couldn't wait until spring. Jed was one of the few people who chose to stay in this country, where he could do the most good. He's a rare man, David."

He picked up the bundle, moved toward the door, and David followed. "Jed can pay me when he gets back. No worry about that. Just you be sure you ride straight home, and get there safely."

They tied the supplies on Betsy's back, behind the saddle, and she waited patiently while David put his foot into the stirrup and sat squarely in place. Mr. Dickins untied the reins, handed them to David and patted him on the knee.

"Now you have your gun, your supplies, everything you need. And as handsome a coat as I ever saw on a mountain man. Are you ready, boy? Can you get back without any trouble?"

David nodded. "Yes, I think so. If I fall asleep, Betsy will keep going. She knows the way."

"I expect she does at that. Well, good luck, boy."

When David had ferried across the river again, and paid the man with powder and bullets, he went only a short way before he stopped to eat his lunch. It was well past noon, to be sure, but he had dipped into the food a few times. Now there was nothing else to think about. He could relax and have a rest.

He sat under a tree while Betsy browsed nearby. A light shower pattered around them, and he was careful to keep his powder horn dry inside his coat. Then he was through with lunch and he climbed back into the saddle, clucked to Betsy, and rode off down the trail.

Betsy trotted easily across the fields and the low hills,

14

through patches of wood, winding in and out with the broad trail. David was sure they would be home by dark. There was no need to hurry. Nothing would happen, he was sure, and about suppertime he would ride up to the cabin, just as he had planned.

In fact, as the afternoon wore on, it seemed to him that he might even take a few minutes to see if he could catch a trout or two. Scat Creek wound in close to the trail not far from here, and he had his fishline with him, hook and all, neatly rolled inside the band of his hat.

He had never fished this far down the creek. He knew there were many wonderful pools just waiting for his hook, and any number of big trout lurking in the deep places, ready to be caught.

They were only a few miles from the cabin when he decided to stop and try his luck. He slid down from Betsy, tied her loosely to a tree by the trail, and shoved his gun under the fastenings of the bundle so it would be safe and dry. Then he cut a slim sapling with his knife, trimmed the leaves from it, tied his line to the end, and hurried down toward the sound of the creek.

He discovered a lovely pool not far away. He went to it carefully, peeking over the grass fringe so he would not frighten any fish there, and saw how the trees hung over it, and how the water curled around a great boulder in the middle. It was there that he would drop his hook, right where the current eddied a little.

A few feet away was a rotting log, the best source of bait. He kicked it apart until he found a fat, white grub, which he fixed on the hook. Cautiously he moved toward the edge of the stream, swung the bait out and into the water, just above the boulder, and watched it drift slowly around, exactly where he wanted it to go.

17

He heard a sound not so far away, a familiar noise of squeaking wheels. An ox cart, probably, being driven down the trail. He wanted to see who it was, but just then there was a sudden surge on the fishline, his pole bobbed down, and he felt the tug of a big trout.

It was almost as though he were trying to hang on to the fish with his bare hands. He could feel every twist and quiver and jerk, and his heart thumped. He would let the fish have its own way for a while. The line might break, or the hook might pull out if he tried to haul it in now.

He watched the fishline switch back and forth, cutting through the water. There was a small beach below, and he gradually maneuvered the trout closer to the shore, pulling on the pole whenever the fish came nearer.

The sound of the ox cart became suddenly louder. There was a crack of a heavy whip, and the hoarse shout of a driver. David hardly dared turn his head long enough to see what was going on. One false move and he might lose the fish. It was probably the biggest one he had ever caught.

He was lucky. The fish drove toward the shore, and he flipped his pole up at the same time. The trout came flying through the air, twisting and shining, and fell almost at his feet.

Then he had to turn to see where the cart was. His mouth opened in surprise. At precisely that moment, he saw two oxen passing close to Betsy, and a man standing with whip and reins, urging them on. The whip drew back, snaked forward across the animals, and cracked with a pop like a gunshot, striking Betsy on the side of her neck. On her wound.

Betsy reared up in sudden terror. While the oxen and the driver rolled past, she pawed the air, lunged back-

18

wards. The reins came loose as though they had not been tied at all. She started to run.

"Betsy! Betsy!"

It was no use calling to her. She streaked off into the woods, back the way they had come, the bundle of supplies bouncing up and down as she disappeared.

He ran to the trail as fast as he could, dragging the fish. The ox cart had lumbered away, too. He saw a movement in an open spot in the trees. It was Betsy, running as hard as she could go.

David let go the fishline, began to chase her. The man with the oxen followed the trail, but Betsy had headed off to the right, and David ran frantically, watching for any sign of her, looking for the bundle or the gun in case they fell off.

He ran for a long time. Finally he had to stop and lean against a tree, his breath coming in great gasps. He had seen nothing. Betsy was gone. And all the things he had bought. And the gun. She would likely keep on running for miles, goaded by the sting of the whip across her wound. There was no use trying to catch her. She was gone. He would have to return without her.

Long after it was dark, a solitary shadow came out of the woods, across a little open patch, and on toward a cabin. There was a light that glowed through an open door. A woman was standing under the dogtrot, a shawl around her shoulders.

She peered into the night, listened.

"David—is that you? David?"

The shadow came closer, slowly, and stopped a few feet away.

"Hello, Mom."

A silence fell between them. Mrs. Carder pulled her shawl tighter.

"I'm glad you got back safe, boy."

"Yes, Mom."

"What's that in your hand?"

He looked down at the limp fish. "I caught it. That's—all I brought home."

"Hmm. Not Betsy. Or the supplies. Or the gun."

"No."

"Well." She turned toward the cabin and paused. "I expect you're ready for supper. Hand me that trout and I'll cook it."

"Mom—I don't think I'd like it. Maybe I could do without supper."

She took the trout and looked at him sternly. "You'll have supper. Trout. Whatever you have to tell me can wait. Right now you're going to eat. Is that clear?"

He sighed and nodded. His shoulders sagged. "All right, Mom."

They walked into the cabin, barred the door behind them, and David shrugged out of his heavy coat, hung it and his cap on a peg, and looked around the room. A warm fire was snapping in the fireplace. He sloshed a dipper of water from the bucket into the tin basin, washed his face and hands hurriedly, dried himself on the towel, and sat down on the bench by the table while his mother quickly cleaned the trout and put it in a pan.

A candle was burning in the middle of the table, and David gazed across it toward his mother. He told her what had happened. She didn't have much to say. But when he was through with his meal, she went to the window and stared into the darkness.

"Son, I remember something your father said once."

"Yes, Mom?"

"Something about growing up. He said it didn't happen all by itself. You have to work at it. And it takes a few days. I expect if Jed were here now he'd say the same thing to you. You think on that, boy. You may take some comfort in it."

When he was in bed that night and the candle was out, David lay awake a long time watching the firelight flicker across the beams above. He listened to the lonely sound of the wind outside, the moan of the high trees. Somewhere off in the night, he thought, miles away, Betsy was standing by herself, listening to the noises around her, afraid, and lonely.

David pulled the blanket up around his neck. "I'm sorry, Betsy," he whispered. "I'm sorry," and the corners of his eyes began to sting.

Chapter 2

The Last Toe

EARLY THE next morning, when the gray of dawn was just beginning to show through the window, they had a visitor. Breakfast was over, the room was warm from the new fire, and David was about to pull on his coat and take care of Rosy, when there was a knock at the door.

Mrs. Carder lifted the latch, opened the door and looked out.

"Morning, ma'am."

"Good morning, sir."

"My name is Cox. I'm combing the countryside for any extra supplies I can find. For the new emigrants, the people coming down river. They're poorly provided for."

The door swung wider. "You come inside, Mr. Cox. We'll see what we can find."

The man came up the step, entered slowly with his hat in his hand and pulled the door shut.

"I'm Mrs. Carder, and this is David. Mr. Carder is not here."

"Ma'am—would that be Jed Carder?"

"It would."

"Well, now." Cox shook his head. "I should have known. One of your neighbors told me his place was hereabouts. But you folks are doing enough already. Jed is helping those people, giving his time—I wouldn't have bothered you, not if I had realized this was Jed's farm."

"Mr. Cox," Mrs. Carder lifted her chin slightly, "how much help is enough help? We'll do what we can. Goodness knows none of us would have gotten far in this country without lots of help from others. Now you just tell me what you're looking for, and we'll see what we have. You mentioned supplies."

"Yes, I did. Almost anything. Flour, bacon, harness, blankets, guns, powder, lead—anything you can spare."

"We are out of flour just now. There's some bacon, a few loaves of bread. Plenty of milk and butter, salt, tea."

The man brought out a little notebook, wrote in it with a stub of a pencil.

"Any guns?"

Mrs. Carder glanced toward David. "No, no guns. Some powder in a horn, some caps and bullets."

"I see. You have a barn. Would you mind if I looked in it?"

"Of course not. We want you to see everything we have."

The three of them walked out under the dogtrot, opened the door to the barn. Rosy was waiting to be let out, and David patted her on the flank while she ambled past the corner of the cabin and found her favorite patch of grass, where she began to eat.

Mr. Cox stepped inside, looked at the tools on the wall, the froe, the mattock, the shovels, the pieces of harness, and the plow on the floor.

"Don't you have a horse, ma'am?"

"No. But we do have some seed. Three sacks of it, over there."

The man went to the sacks, pulled one open and stuck his hand inside. "It's good seed. You'll be needing that for planting pretty soon."

"Yes, but we can share it."

Mr. Cox made another entry in his notebook. He glanced around. "I think that's all I want to see," he said, and walked out of the barn. He turned toward Mrs. Carder and David as they came out. "Ma'am, you're all alone here."

"Yes, David and I."

"You're a long way from the settlement. No close neighbors."

Mrs. Carder smiled gently. "What are you saying, Mr. Cox? That it's not safe for us here?"

He nodded. "Where can you go for help? If a band of renegade Indians came through, or anything happened, what would you do? It looks to me as though you ought to move down with your neighbors, and live with them until Jed gets back."

"The Griffins?"

"Yes, I think that would be wise."

"I'm sure you mean to give us good advice," she said softly, "but it's our job to stay on the farm and take care of it. Jed expects us to do that—unless it gets so we can't manage at all. Besides, we aren't so far from neighbors. You must have forgotten about the man on the next claim."

24

"Do you mean Martin?"

"That's right. He's a good neighbor, friendly, and ready to help us out. We can call on him if we have to."

Mr. Cox shook his head. "Not any more," he said. "He told me to tell you. He said he was sorry, but he made up his mind."

"About what, Mr. Cox?"

"Martin left. Last evening. I talked to him just before he rode away for Sacramento. He's gone to the gold-fields."

He gazed at both of them. "I'm sorry to bring you bad news. But that's why I mentioned the Griffins, and thought you should move there. It's not safe here. Besides, there's nothing to be done here, even with those sacks of seed."

"Sir?"

"You have no horse, Mrs. Carder. You couldn't plow."

She pressed her lips together just a little. "We appreciate your concern, Mr. Cox," she said. "We're obliged to you for the message from Martin. Now if you'll let us know what supplies you need from us, we will be happy to give you whatever you want."

The man looked down at the ground a moment, then glanced at David. "Boy," he said, "can I have a look at your powder horn?"

David got it quickly from the house, handed it and the sack of bullets to Mr. Cox. The man pulled out the cap of the horn, looked inside. He took his own horn, shook black powder from it until David's was full to the brim. He tamped the lid back in place.

"Here, son," he said, and handed it to him. "You just hold this for me while I climb on my horse." He went to his mount, took down his gun and prepared to swing up

25

into the saddle. "Here—if you'll hold this for me a moment, David, I'd appreciate it."

David took them as the man rose into the saddle. Without another word, Cox clucked his tongue, flipped the reins, touched the brim of his hat, and rode away from the cabin.

"Mr. Cox—" David held up the gun and the powder horn. "Mr. Cox!"

But the man did not stop. As he turned into the woods, a small piece of paper fluttered to the ground. And then he was gone.

David ran after him, found the scrap of paper, and picked it up. He stared after the man. There was no doubt about it; he was not coming back. David walked slowly to his mother, studied the note and handed it to her. "Here, Mom. I can't read it very well."

She took it from him. "You're going to learn to read better," she said. "And to cipher. I've been worrying about that."

David groaned. "What does it say?"

She glanced at it, slowly crumpled it in her palm. "It's the list he made, son. It says we have a cow, no flour, a few pieces of harness, three sacks of seed. No horse. And no gun. That's all it says."

David held up the gun. "He forgot it. He didn't come back for it."

She nodded. "He didn't forget. He's a kindly sort, David. I expect he thinks we need it more than those emigrants. And maybe he's right. Maybe he's right about the other, too."

David shook his head quickly. "No, Mom. Not if you mean about moving down with the Griffins. You don't get along with them. Neither do I. I don't like them."

"You mind your speech, young man," she said, but there was no scolding in her voice. "They're our neighbors, and neighbors are hard to come by in this country."

"But we don't have to live with them."

"It wouldn't be easy, son. Just the same, we might not have a choice. There are wild animals, and Indians. And not even Martin to go to for help. Jed wouldn't want us to stay. I don't think he would."

David straightened up, rested the gun on the toe of his boot. "He told us to take care of the farm until he got back."

"I know your father's mind better. He'd want us to be safe. I don't care to leave either, boy. But it's not as simple as that. I'll think on it. I'll have to make up my mind. Maybe in a few days."

"Mom—let's wait until the last minute. Until we have to. We've got a gun now. We'll get food somewhere. We've got plenty of vegetable seed for a garden, and I'll build a fence. Maybe when it's time to sow those three sacks of grain we'll have a horse."

She smiled at him. "Tell you what, boy," she said, "you start on your fence. Maybe things will look different in a few days. You start on it, David."

He didn't wait for her to reconsider. He loaded the gun, put it on the pegs over the fireplace, filled the water keg at the creek and carried it into the cabin, made sure Rosy was all right, and then started to think about his fence.

He went into the barn, where the tools were hanging on the wall. There was an auger, a bucksaw, a hatchet, a drawknife, a mallet, and a froe. He took down the froe and the mallet, carried them to the chopping block, picked up the pole ax, and started across the clearing.

A little study gave him an idea of how many sections

27

there should be. He could decide that better afterwards. The main business now was to cut poles and split stakes. And that would be no problem.

He always liked splitting shakes from cedar bolts, hammering the heavy blade of the froe into the end of a section of dry wood, working the blade in a little, shoving it and prying it until a thin board, beautifully red and yellowish, split off with a single, clean snapping noise. But this time he would make posts. It would be harder to do.

He found the tumble of cedar bolts off in the woods, where they had used them before, and there he went to work, pounding and prying until he had a pile of good straight posts. This would do to get started. If he needed more, he would make them. For the poles, he walked toward the creek where there was a grove of alders that grew slim and tall with scarcely any branches on them. They would be limber, but they were about the right size. Besides, he liked to cut alder. The ax bit into the wood cleanly and it took only a few chops to bring one down, then a single hard blow to cut it off square at the slim end.

He carried all his posts and poles back to the clearing, laboring hard and steadily until he had a great pile. He studied it a moment, his hands on his hips. It would be a solid fence. Rugged, neat, and trim.

He laid out the poles around the clearing. There were not enough to go around; in fact, he had only half enough, so he put them along an end and down the side away from the cabin. He'd do that much to begin with. He was anxious to get some of the fence together.

He sharpened each post, then took one and jabbed it hard into the ground, pressed and wobbled it until it was low enough to hit on the end. The poleax was good for hammering. One side of the head was a blade, and the other side was flat. He swung the ax again and again until the post was just right. He used a pole to measure with, stuck in another post, hammered with all his strength, and soon there was a line of posts—not exactly in a straight row, but fairly straight, and very solid. The next step would be the poles. It wasn't going to take long at all.

There was a difficulty, though. A small one. How to fasten the poles to the posts. He picked up a length of slim alder, hoisted it into position, and studied the problem. There were a few nails on the farm, but not enough. Besides, the square nails were too valuable. And they always bent whenever he tried to hammer them. Nails wouldn't do. Maybe he could tie the poles in place. Still, he had no rawhide thongs.

It was very irritating that such a little problem should stand in the way. He tried to think of some other way to put it together. But he couldn't think of one. Not right now. He dropped the pole, kicked at it, walked over to the chopping block and sat down.

He looked up at the rafters above him. His old fishing pole was there, the line drooping in a long curve. Maybe if he went fishing he would be able to think things through. Besides, he would be getting food, and that was important.

He stood on the block, reached up and pulled down the pole, saw that the hook was in order, and glanced across the clearing. He could dig some worms. It would be a fine way to spend the rest of the day. There was one pool in particular where he would be sure to catch something. He got down, started to walk away with the pole in his hand.

"David."

He stopped, turned around. Mrs. Carder was standing on the step to the cabin. "Where are you off to, young man?"

"I'm going fishing."

"You're not going fishing."

"But Mom—"

"Right now it's time for lunch. After that, there's a small matter of book learning."

David groaned. "Reading?"

She nodded. "Since you don't seem to be getting on with the fence, the next most important thing is schooling."

"We have to eat, Mom. I can catch some trout."

"Yes, and we have to feed our heads, too. Or do you think you have a head just to chew with? Maybe you want to turn into a full-grown boy that can't read or write or figure—"

"Like Dan Griffin?"

"I didn't say any name. I only said you're going to learn a few things." She moved back into the cabin. He climbed slowly onto the chopping block again, stuck the pole into the rafters, and walked into the cabin.

There was a plate of food on the table. And beside it was an old, worn book. One he had seen many times. He sat down while his mother stirred something in the iron kettle hanging in the fireplace.

"It smells good," he said, looking up at the ceiling. "Stew?"

She glanced at him. "Hmm," she said. "Did you imagine we would have something else? We're lucky we had a scrap of bacon for it."

"Oh, it's fine, Mom. I just meant it would be good to

have a mess of trout now and then. When we needed a change, maybe."

She banged her wooden spoon on the rim of the kettle. "Indeed. When the time comes we have to choose between eating or studying your lessons, you can go fishing. But when the choice is between stew with study, or fish without study, then we eat stew. And mighty good stew at that."

He began to eat. It was good stew, at that, and before long he set the spoon in the empty bowl and pushed back his chair.

"Just a minute," said Mrs. Carder. She came over to the table, opened the book, and placed it in front of him. "Now. You haven't tackled this for some time. Maybe it will go better today. Start with the title page, and then we'll skip over a few leaves. Go ahead."

He bent over, squinted at the words, and read: "Journal of an Exploring Tour. By the Reverend Samuel Parker. 1838. Mom, this book's pretty old. It was printed about eleven years ago."

"Never mind." She flipped over several pages, and the book lay flat because the binding was so loose. "Maybe you don't know it, boy, but this book had quite a bit to do with our coming out here. Mr. Parker painted a mighty attractive picture, and your father pored over this book by the hour back in Missouri. And it's still good reading. Now you start here, son."

Slowly, following the words with his finger, David read line after line, pausing to sound out the hard words, and gradually he worked his way to the bottom of the page and turned it over.

It made him think of their trip west, two years ago. Of the long stretches and the flat prairies, the slow oxen and

31

the creaking wheels, the rain storms, the troubles, and the good times. They had left the oxen and the wagon far up the Columbia River and traveled down by boats, and later his father had traded the animals.

He read on, came to a hard word, and stopped. He waited for his mother to prompt him, but her mind was far away, and he lifted his head to look at her. His eyes swept to the window. He had seen something, only half a glimpse of a face—

He jumped up suddenly.

"David—what's wrong?"

"Mom—I saw a face at the window. An Indian."

"What?" She went to the window, looked out this way and that. "Are you sure? I don't see anybody." She turned to stare at him. "Why, what are you going to do? Why do you have your knife out?"

He had his knife in his hand and was holding it with the blade down. He put a finger to his lips, and went to the door, took hold of the latch.

"I saw him, Mom."

"David—now you be careful, boy. Don't you take any chances, hear?"

He opened the door, slid out quietly, and glanced around. He moved to the right, looked along the cabin. Quickly he hunched over, ran down the side of the building, peered around the corner, and went back to the dog-trot. There was nothing. No sign of anybody.

He glanced at the barn. The door was ajar. Maybe he had left it that way. He wasn't sure. He walked to it, paused in the doorway, and looked.

Nothing. Everything was in its place, nothing was disturbed. Except for one thing, and he stared at it a long time before he realized what it was. It was a toe. A brown toe that stuck out in the open, at the edge of the seed sacks. As though someone had slid in behind them and hidden himself—all but that last toe.

He clutched his knife tight, crept over to the sacks until he could lean forward and catch hold of the last one. Then he pulled it back, hard, and raised the knife to strike.

Chapter 3

The Missing Gun

FOR A moment he stayed just as he was, the knife in the air, his eyes wide, his arm ready—and then his hand came slowly down. He blinked.

There was a boy looking up at him, an Indian with straight black hair hanging down the sides of his face, and two dark eyes that stared calmly back.

David tried to think of some Chinook words. "Nika mika tillicum. You Kloash Indian?"

The boy did not reply.

"What are you doing here?"

"Hiding."

"Hiding? From what?"

The Indian brought out a hand, jerked a thumb toward the cabin. "A couple of settlers. They've been chasing me. They almost caught me. And they're probably almost here now."

"What are they chasing you for?"

The boy closed his eyes and raised his brows. He sighed. "I'd rather tell you about it later. When I have more time. Right now all I want is a chance to hide. I'm tired." He glanced up at David. "Why don't you just forget I'm here? Just until they leave?"

There was a call from across the clearing, a loud hallo, and a man yelling their name: "Carder! Mrs. Carder! There's an Indian around here. Lock your door!"

David turned, saw his mother step out of the cabin, look quickly in at him, and then move toward the man who was warning them.

"Well," said the Indian, "I'll let you make up your own mind. Either you tell them, or you don't. I'm going to stay right here, and see which you do. I'll let you decide."

David hesitated only a moment. He shoved the sack of seed back against the boy. "You hunch down," he said. "Pull yourself in there. Don't move."

He heard the man coming closer, heard him talk with his mother, and saw that they were walking directly toward the barn. He only had time to straighten up and quickly kick a piece of burlap over the toe that was still exposed, before faces appeared in the doorway.

It was Mr. Griffin and his son, Dan.

The man was panting heavily, and the sweat stood on his face. His eyes seemed smaller and beadier than David remembered them.

"Boy—have you seen an Indian? Did he come around here?"

David put his knife back in his pocket and moved to the doorway.

"Sir? An Indian?"

Mr. Griffin banged a fist on the side of the building.

"Blast it, boy, you heard me. I said have you seen an Indian here? Did he come this way? We saw him head across the clearing, right for your buildings—he must be here somewhere—did you see him or not?"

"Is he dangerous, sir?"

"Dangerous! Of course he's dangerous. He's a thief. We saw him steal. He's a murdering, tricky Indian, and Dan here saw him steal our property and make off with it. Now, did you see him?"

David shook his head slowly. "I'm sorry," he said, "but I didn't see any dangerous Indians."

"You sure?"

"Yes, sir. I'd let you know in a minute."

Dan narrowed his eyes and tried to crowd past David into the barn. "Maybe he's hiding in here, Paw. I'll just poke around and see—"

David stood right where he was and put his hands on his hips. Dan bent toward him. "Why don't you let me by, Dave Carder? Why don't you let me in there so I can make sure?"

David looked up into his face. He did not move.

"I answered your question," said David. "There's no call for you to bother. I told you what you wanted to know, didn't I?"

"I guess so. But suppose he hid in here?"

"This is our barn, Dan Griffin, and I know what's in it. Now you just back on out of here and get on his trail. If he headed this way, he's probably hightailing it up Scat Creek. Maybe he's half a mile away by now. Why don't you start running if you're so set on catching him?"

Dan glared at him. Slowly he turned toward his father. A look passed between them, and they moved out under the dogtrot.

"Mrs. Carder—you sure your boy is telling the truth?"

An icy smile came to her lips. "Mr. Griffin," she said softly, "I don't believe I understood you rightly. I don't believe you meant to say what I thought I heard. Did you now?"

"Ma'am?"

"You asked if Davy was telling the truth. Did you mean to say that?"

His face flushed quickly and he waved his hands in the air while he groped for words. "Did I mean to say that? No, I guess not. I don't know what I meant. Only—it does seem funny we traced that thief this far and he gave us the slip right around here."

"Mr. Griffin," said David.

"Eh—what, boy?"

"What did he steal from you?"

"He stole property, that's what. Something that belonged to us."

"What was the property?"

Griffin rubbed his jaw clumsily with his hand, glanced from David to Mrs. Carder. "He stole," he said in a small voice, "a pie. An apple pie."

An awkward silence followed. Nobody said a word, and "apple pie" seemed to hang in the air all by itself. Finally the man turned roughly on Dan. "You come with me. We're still going to look for him. If he headed up the creek he's gotten clean away by now, but we're going to take a look. Get moving, Dan."

"I'm going, Paw," said Dan in an irritated voice, and together they walked away, around the corner of the cabin, and into the woods toward Scat Creek.

David watched until he could see them no more before he looked at his mother. Mrs. Carder's gaze was fixed steadily on him. She was not smiling.

"The truth comes hard sometimes," she said. "But I've never had reason to think you weren't man enough to abide by it. I don't mistrust you now, either."

He looked straight back into her eyes. "No, ma'am. I told him the truth."

"You said no Indians."

"I said no dangerous Indians. There's an Indian in there all right, but he's not dangerous. He's just a boy."

"Hmm. Sounds like twisty talk to me. Maybe you changed the meaning by not saying 'dangerous' harder than the other words." Her expression softened. "But I expect under the circumstances you weren't obliged to reveal any more than you had to. Mr. Griffin and his boy were not being sensible. No telling what they might have done if they'd laid hands on your Indian. A thief they called him and worse."

"He said he'd explain it all to me after they left."

She shook her head sadly. "People have a hard time thinking straight, boy. I wonder if they'll ever learn."

A quiet voice spoke from the doorway of the barn then, and David and his mother turned to see the Indian boy standing there.

"Thank you for letting me hide," he said. "I was going to ask if I could work or something to pay him for the pie. The trouble was I ate it first. I was hungry. I couldn't wait. Then they couldn't wait. So I had to run."

David studied the boy's face, his long hair. He had a good coat, though it was torn, rough trousers, but no shoes.

"What were you doing around the Griffins' place? What made you come through this part of the country?"

The boy laughed. His eyes suddenly sparkled.

38

"I live here, mister. This is my home. From the Willamette River to the Pacific Ocean. Always has been."

"We've never seen you before."

"I've been at the mission school. I was going back to my tribe. They—"

He stopped in the middle of his sentence. He was staring past them, at the corner of the cabin. David and his mother turned, and they saw, too.

There, leaning against the side of the log house, listening and watching with smiles on their faces, were two figures. Mr. Griffin and Dan.

"So," said the man. "You did lie to us after all. You said he wasn't hiding here. And he was, all the time."

Mrs. Carder folded her arms and lifted her chin.

"We did not lie to you. But, may Heaven help me, if I'd had to conceal the truth to protect this lad from you, sir, I would have been sorely tempted. It appears to me that you have put us in this position by being so unreasonable, by persecuting this boy, chasing him before he could explain. And what would you have done if you'd caught him? Killed him? Is that what you wanted to do?"

"No ma'am. Not quite. Just teach him a lesson, that's all. Give him a good thrashing he wouldn't forget."

"Indeed. A thrashing for being hungry, I suppose."

"For stealing. He's an Indian, don't forget that. He has to be taught a few things." He came a step closer. "If you'll just step aside, I'll take this rascal off your hands right now. I'll give him his first lesson."

Mrs. Carder held her ground. When she spoke, her voice was low and tense. "I'll give you five minutes to get off our land, sir," she said.

The man gaped at her in amazement. "Do you mean that? Are you ordering us off your farm?"

"Five minutes. And I mean to stand by it. We have a gun, Mr. Griffin. It's loaded, and I believe I can pull the trigger. I'll take a chance on aiming it. I don't want to have to use it, but if I have to, I will."

The two Griffins began to step backwards, their faces pale. They paused at the corner of the cabin, and the man hunched toward them and wagged a finger.

"All right. We'll go. But you're cutting yourself off from your neighbors. There's nobody else anywhere around here. If you need help, or a place to go, you just remember that. Go ask your Indian friends to save you. Don't come begging to us. You understand what I mean?"

Mrs. Carder gazed steadily at him.

"Four minutes," she said softly.

The two Griffins turned and ran, around the cabin, across the clearing, and faded into the shadows of the woods beyond.

David looked at his mother, studied the side of her face, the clean lines of her jaw and her chin.

"Mom," said he, "they didn't wait to see if you meant it."

"I'm afraid I meant it, when I said it. Seems like when things come to a crisis and you know what's right, you don't have any choice. You do what you feel you have to."

41

She glanced at David. "I wonder what your father would say about this?"

David smiled. "He'd say you did the right thing. If he was here he'd maybe have acted different. But he'd hold by what you said. I know he would."

"You lost your neighbors, Mrs. Carder," said the Indian. "I don't think you can turn to them for help now."

"Help from whom, boy?" she said. "Indians like you? And mountain lions? It begins to look like we need more protection from neighbors. But—we can't settle these problems, not right now. Anyway, Mr. David, you have a job to finish."

"A job, Mom?"

"Certainly. Your reading lesson. Remember? Now you and your friend get on inside and see how much of that book you can read. I have a mind things will go faster."

She was right. When David and the Indian boy, whose name was Sam Skookum, sat down at the table to read the book, it soon became evident that Sam was a scholar. His years at the mission school had taught him to read very well. For a while he just listened, until David asked for help. Then Sam began to read, and both David and his mother listened for page after page, missing scarcely a word.

After a while the boys stopped, and just sat and looked at the fire. Sam stuck his feet toward the flames, spread his toes, slouched down, and got comfortable.

"I threw away my shoes," he said. "Couldn't run fast enough in them when your neighbors got after me. They never did fit, anyway, always made blisters. I'm looking forward to getting home, and putting on a pair of moccasins, and going fishing."

David glanced at his mother, and back to Sam. "You mean you can go fishing whenever you want to?"

"No. But I had to get out of that school. I got tired of sitting at a desk and cramming my head full. There was another reason I left, I guess. It isn't easy being an Indian and living around settlers. Too many people like the Griffins." He yawned. "It felt like a good time to take a vacation, and maybe fish, too." He got up. "Mrs. Carder, is the reading lesson over? Can I have a look around the place?"

"Yes, it's over. In fact, we did more this afternoon than we usually do. You two go outside while I do my work. I'll be glad to have you both out of the way for a while."

They went out, walked into the barn, talked, and wandered over into the clearing. Sam saw the posts and poles.

"What are you making? A bear trap?"

"No. A fence. At least I was until I ran into trouble. We don't have anything to put it together with. Not enough nails."

"Nails," said Sam. "Lots of things were put together in this country without nails. My father, the chief, made a fence once. It's still standing. And hard to get through. Solid as can be."

"Did he tie it together?"

"No. He made a little auger. Bored holes. Hammered wooden pins through the posts and the poles. It took lots of time and patience, and lots of whittling, but it turned out to be quite a fence. Too bad you don't have an auger."

"We do," said David quietly.

"Of course you could cut more posts and set them up like X's, and let the poles rest where they cross. You'd have to cut more posts. You'd need more cedar."

"We have plenty."

"Then you don't need nails. You can put it together any way you like. Without nails."

43

"But I didn't know about pegs. And X's. Somebody has to tell you about things. You can't just make them up."

Sam laughed. "You can if you give yourself time to think about it. It's like the story the chief told me once. About the first Indian, and a cedar log that had been lying on the ground for a thousand years. The Indian wanted to make a path where the log was, and he came to the log and said, 'Get up, log. Move over. Let me by.' But the log wouldn't move. So the Indian took his knife and cut down a piece of stiff wood and tied a strip of rawhide from one end to the other, and split off a piece of the log and shot it into the air. 'Now, log,' he said, 'I want you to fly away like that.' But the log wouldn't budge.

"The Indian sat down and thought hard, for about a month. Then he got a stone ax and some fire and some sharp shells, and he burned and chopped and scraped at a piece of the log until it was a canoe. He got in it and paddled around in the water and came back and stood over the log. 'Log,' he said, 'that's what I want you to do.' But the log still didn't move. By that time the Indian was getting pretty mad. But he sat down and thought for another couple of months. Then he took his tools and chopped the log into strips, stuck them in holes in the ground and put pegs in the tops and put a roof of bark over it. 'Now, log,' he said, 'you listen to me. You forced me to invent a bow and arrow, and you made me discover canoes. Just for that, you can stand up for the rest of your life and keep the rain off me. How do you like that, log?' But of course there wasn't any log left by then because the Indian had used it up making the first house."

David looked at Sam, and the Indian rubbed his right foot over his left shin. "Is that an old story, Sam?"

"No. I think the chief made it up to show me you can

discover lots of things by yourself, if you take time to figure them out." He glanced at David. "You suppose your mother would mind if I stayed here another day? Maybe between us we could see how to make that fence of yours go together."

David didn't mind at all, nor did Mrs. Carder. After Rosy was milked and put back in the barn, and after they had eaten supper, they all sat around the fireplace again and talked about what it was like in Sam's village on a little bay where a river came down and flowed into the ocean. It sounded like a wonderful place. David hadn't seen the ocean yet, but his father had promised to take him there when they had the time.

The next morning, they went to work on the fence. David got the auger and began boring holes as though he expected to finish the job in an hour. Sam rubbed the side of his jaw, inspected the poles, took the auger, and studied it. They talked about it. They decided that slanting holes for pegs would be better. The poles could rest on pegs.

It seemed like a slow process. They worked a while, stopped and talked, planned their work. But by noon, they had put together one side of the fence, and had started on the end section.

For lunch they had hot tea and corn cakes. Then they went down in the woods to cut more material. Finally, by the time Rosy had to be milked, there stood the fence, all finished. Mrs. Carder came outside to look. David banged the poles with his hands, grasped the posts and tried to shake them. It was all solid, all pegged together with wooden pins as tight as could be, except for one place where the poles slid aside for a gate.

"David Carder," said his mother, "you and Sam have

built a beautiful fence. I don't know how you managed. It's neat, and straight, and strong as can be. Seems to me I heard you talking most of the time. How did you have time for work?"

David laughed. "I don't know. I guess we just talked that fence into place."

There wasn't much for supper that evening. Mrs. Carder made no explanations, and David said nothing. There wasn't any meat. Sam seemed happy enough. And sleepy. There was little talk after their meal. The room was warm and comfortable, they had done a good day's work, and all three of them were ready to go to bed early, even before the light had entirely faded outdoors. David lay awake for a while, listening to the snapping of the fire and staring up at the flickering light.

He knew they would have to have more food soon. To-morrow. Maybe, after Sam was gone, he and his mother would have to talk about what they were going to do. About leaving the place. They couldn't go to the Griffins' place. But they would have to do something.

It was cold and barely dawn when David woke in the morning. He glanced around the room, at the huddle of blankets under the window, then over toward his mother. Her head lifted, and she stared back at him. And at Sam's bed.

It was empty.

"Davy—did you hear him leave?"

David got up, began pulling on his clothes, shivering the while.

"No, Mom, I didn't hear a sound. I didn't know he left."

"Quiet people, Indians," she said. "I wonder if he'll be back."

David built the fire, finding glowing coals in the center of the gray ashes and blowing until there was enough flame to catch the dry twigs he piled on. His mother went about getting breakfast.

Sam still had not shown up when they sat down for their hot porridge. They started to eat in silence, and David poked with his spoon at his milk pudding.

"I didn't think he'd leave without telling us."

Mrs. Carder shook her head. "Nor I, son."

"You don't think he hates us because we're settlers, too? Like the Griffins?"

"We gave him no reason to feel that way. I'm sure he felt friendly toward us yesterday. He's not likely to change that much overnight."

David ate a mouthful, looked around the room, at the fireplace, at the silent clock on the mantel, the one his parents had brought out all the way from Missouri, the one that never ran. And he glanced up at the pegs where he had put the gun.

He put down his spoon suddenly.

"Mom."

"Davy—what's wrong?"

"The gun, Mom. Look. It's gone."

She turned to look. There was no gun resting on the pegs above the mantel.

"Did you move it, boy? Are you sure it was there?"

He nodded. "It was. I remember last night when we were sitting here, I looked up and saw it. The light reflected on the hammer. I didn't move it."

"Now, son, let's not jump to conclusions too fast. Let's

49

take one thing at a time. To begin with, we know we can trust Sam, don't we?"

David nodded.

"Even if he took Mrs. Griffin's apple pie—we know why that happened."

"Yes. But he was going home. Maybe he needed the gun."

"Son, either we trust him or we don't. I say, if he took it, he had a good reason. Don't you think we can rely on that?"

David nodded slowly. "I guess we can. I just don't understand. It wasn't right for him to leave and take the gun—and the powder horn, and the bullets. We need them, too."

Mrs. Carder had nothing more to say, and he lowered his head and went on with his meal. When he was through, he went out to take care of Rosy, and let her browse by the new fence. It was a good fence, but it gave him no joy.

It was around noontime, when they were sitting inside with the door closed, that they both heard the noise. It was a quiet sort of sound, a heavy plump followed by one distinct, clear knock. They stared at each other, and David rose from his bench. He walked to the door, opened it just a crack and looked out. Slowly he opened the door wider, stepped down, and stared at what was lying on the hewn step. He raised his head and peered all around. Nothing. Not a sign of anybody.

But on the step—

"Mom, you come out here and see for yourself. Look what's here!"

She came to the doorway and gasped. There, leaning

50

against the cabin was the gun, the powder horn and the pouch hanging from the ramrod. And stretched across the step was the carcass of a freshly cleaned deer, a small one, stuffed with ferns.

"David—why, that's enough meat for days. Now how do you suppose he managed to track down that animal?"

"He's an Indian, remember? He just borrowed the gun long enough to pay us back with food. But—why didn't he tell us what he was going to do?"

Mrs. Carder shook her head happily. "I don't know. Or maybe I do know. He wanted it to be a present, and a good surprise. Maybe he's watching us right now from somewhere off in the woods, laughing at how surprised we are. Well, now. I'm glad we trusted him after all, aren't you?"

"Of course."

"And now we have food. And the gun. We don't have to leave. Not quite yet."

"No."

"Hmm. There's another side to this, Davy."

"What?"

"You know what this will do to your fishing?"

"What do you mean?"

"You won't have to worry so much about catching trout. You can spend more time on your lessons."

"My lessons!"

"Yes, boy. You can get on with your reading."

"Huh!" He turned around, stared toward the woods, looking for somebody who was nowhere in sight. "That Sam Skookum!" he said. "I wish he'd stayed around just a little longer. Just long enough for me to tell him what I think of him. Huh!"

Chapter 4

Mystery of the Clock

SOMETIME DURING the night, it began to rain. Slowly at first, a scattering of heavy drops that fell like small marbles on the roof. Then more. And more. Before long it turned into such a loud and steady drumming that David awoke and sat up in the middle of his bed and stared around him in the darkness.

His ears filled with the sound, a rushing, rattling and hammering that grew louder and heavier. His mother woke, too.

"Davy—what on earth is all that racket? Is it rain?"

"It must be. It couldn't be anything else. But I never heard it rain as hard as this." He got out of bed, went to the window and pressed his face against the pane. It was too dark to see a thing. Outdoors it was black as black.

He crossed to the door, opened it a little and stuck his face out the crack. The rain was roaring, and he could see it coming down off the dogtrot in sheets. He shut the door quickly, thought about the fire in the fireplace, and crouched down by the hearth. He blew hard on the embers. He heard the irregular plop! plop! fizz! as the rain came down the flue.

A red patch glowed, burst into flame, and he put together a few pieces on the edge of the hearth where the water would not quench them. His mother went to the window, and by then there was enough firelight to glisten on the water tumbling off the eaves, and she tsk-tsk'd and shook her head.

"Davy, this isn't just a rain. This is a cloudburst. This is the kind of downpour that can turn creeks into rivers and trails into ditches, and wash out whole fields if it keeps up."

"It can't keep up, Mom. There isn't enough water in the whole sky to keep coming down that hard. It will have to stop pretty soon."

But it didn't. It poured straight down out of the night sky, thundering steadily onto the roof of the cabin without letting up a bit. A pool formed in the back of the fireplace and spread until the fire was burning on a little island of ashes, and they had to soak up the water with rags before it crept into the room. They thought about the sacks of seed at the same moment. David went out into the night, feeling his way to the barn, past Rosy, and groped over to the bags. They were up off the ground and dry. He pulled an old tarpaulin down off a rafter and covered them to make sure.

Under the dogtrot, the rain had made a little stream crossing from one side to the other, and he stepped in the middle of it. It was deep enough to come to his ankles. He stood there a few minutes to listen to the loudness of the downpour, and to watch the vague shadows of the water rolling off the shakes, before he went into the cabin again and tended the fire.

After a while they went back to bed and fell asleep in spite of the sound. And they did not awaken until long past dawn, because it was almost impossible to tell that daylight had come. It was still raining hard.

Even Rosy didn't want to go out into the weather. She stood under the roof between the barn and the cabin, only now and then venturing out to search for grass, and coming back to stand while she chewed and gazed soberly at the rain.

David thought he should investigate things. He got his father's old waxed raincoat and oiled hat and set out past the fence, down the path that led through the clearing and toward the alders by the creek. Beyond the stream, and stretching up a little valley, was the field they would seed in grain later. He thought he would take one look at it to make sure it was still there, though it would be hard to see, the air was so clouded with falling rain.

There was some protection under the trees along the creek. He stopped and looked at the stream in amazement. It was twice as wide and deep as it should be. It was almost a river, coursing rapidly over the stones and between the banks, and was almost as high as the banks.

A terrible thought struck him. He went down a way, down to where he could see the beaver's dam, and he hung on to a slim tree trunk while he leaned far over to peer through the bushes.

The dam was gone.

Where the beaver dam had extended across the arm of the creek like a dike, all chewed sticks and mud, and had held the water back for the quiet little pool, there was

54

now only the curling, frothy water twisting through the rocks and ferns. Only a handful of white sticks, short and pointed, hung along the edge of the water. The dam had gone, and the pond behind it had disappeared.

It was a dead, desolate picture. The rain coming down through the branches, the roiling water of Scat Creek, the pathetic bits of the dam, and the muddy place behind it. Poor beaver. His home was gone. All his work was destroyed.

David walked back toward the cabin. It wouldn't seem the same along the creek. As long as he could remember, back to the first time he had come here, the dam had been there, and there had been the warning sound of the beaver's tail, and he had come to feel he always had a friend down here in the woods. A friend that he never saw.

The rain did lessen a little as he crossed the clearing. It didn't pelt down so hard. The noise gently faded. By the time he came to the cabin and stood under the dogtrot roof knocking the water off his arms, there was no doubt about it. His mother came through the doorway and stood beside him, gazing out at the green, shining world around them.

"I do believe it's easing up, son."

He nodded. "Yes. But it's too late now."

"Why, son?"

"The beaver dam. It's gone. Washed out. Nothing left of it at all."

"Hmm. Mighty hard thing to happen to the little fellow. But I expect he'll build it again."

"It will take a long time, Mom. He'll have to cut down every stick with his teeth, and chew it into just the right length, and float it into the water, and work and work

55

until it holds again. I don't know if he'll ever have the heart to do it all."

Mrs. Carder smiled. "Well, now, son, let's just wait and see. Maybe we just have to figure that the beaver is braver than that. It might be that it takes more than a broken dam to make him quit. Don't you think so?"

"It would take more stubbornness than I have."

"I don't think he'll give up easily. Let's wait and see."

Inside the cabin it was gloomy. David put more wood on the fire and hung his wet clothes in front of it, draped over the back of the rocking chair, and Mrs. Carder went to work in her kitchen.

David sat at the table and looked around the room. It was quieter now, since the rain had finally turned into a drizzle, and the only noise was the snapping of vine maple in the fire, and his mother's spoon knocking on a wooden bowl. He looked up at the mantel and the old clock sitting there. Its hands were pointing to eight o'clock, as they had as long as he could remember.

"Mom, how old is that clock?"

"The clock? Land sakes, I don't know. It used to belong to your grandfather. The last thing he said before he died was for me to take care of it. He wanted to tell me something else about it, but then it was too late. I never understood why it was so important, but I've kept it. Bringing it west on the trip was not easy. All those miles, and that heavy clock—when it was in the wagon, I didn't mind so much. But at the river we had to come down in those canoes. You remember that. I held it in my arms most of the time. And the ride up here to the claim—it was a chore, bringing that clock."

"Why doesn't it run?"

"It used to, son. It kept good time. But your grandfather kept it in shape. He was a patient man."

"Mom—"

"Yes?"

"Can I fix it?"

Mrs. Carder stopped working, turned around and gazed at David, then at the clock, and at him again. She thought for a moment.

"I'll make a bargain with you, Davy."

"Yes'm. A bargain?"

She nodded. "I'll let you work on that clock if you can show me how many times each wheel turns in twenty-four hours."

David jumped up with a shout. "Hurray!" Suddenly he became quiet again, and looked at her strangely. "Mom, that sounds like arithmetic."

"Yes, it does, doesn't it? Well—is it a bargain, son?"

"Hmm. All right. But I'll have to work on it for a long time just to find out about the wheels."

"Of course you will. You just go ahead. You can have the whole table to put it on. I think it will do you both good, you and the clock, too."

It was heavy, as David found when he lifted it off the mantel. He grasped its sides, lifted it down against his chest and it made a faint jangling and bumping while he carried it to the table and set it facing the window. He unlatched the long door that was glass above and metal mirror below.

Carefully he took off the hands, the wooden face with its gold curlicues in the corners, laying the pieces down flat. Next he took out the two weights, and gently removed the pendulum.

There were little pins to hold the works in place. Slowly, carefully, he removed them, and lifted out the movement. He studied it for a long time before he decided he had to take it all apart. And that took time. It wasn't until late in the afternoon that all the parts of the clock, the wooden wheels, the cords for the weights, the brass pendulum ball, everything, was laid neatly before him.

"My land," said his mother. "Are you sure you haven't taken on too big a job? You think you can get all that together again?"

He nodded. "I know I can. There's a place for each piece, and it will go together only one way. I put every bit down just as I took it out, all in order."

"Well. Do you know how it works?"

"I think so," and he proceeded to tell her, until she turned back to her work, shaking her head.

"Davy. How many times—"

"—does each wheel turn?"

"Yes."

"I'll have to figure that out."

"All right. Take your time, son. I'll wait."

It was a long wait. They ate supper in front of the fire, holding their plates on their laps in order not to disturb the pieces on the table. Then David went back to stare at the wheels, touching one, picking up another, studying it, counting the cogs painfully while he tried to find his answers.

He went to bed that night without solving the problem. He put his arms under his head and looked up at the ceiling before he slept. All he could see was wheels, clock wheels, and hundreds of cogs bristling on their rims. Even when he closed his eyes, he saw them. All night long, it seemed, they were in his dreams, slowly turning, this one twice as fast as that one, the next one three times as fast, the cogs going by one at a time while he counted them.

In the morning he awoke suddenly and jumped out of bed onto the cold floor.

"I've got it!" he said.

Mrs. Carder raised her head and blinked at him.

"You've got what, boy?"

"I know how to do it now. I thought about it all night —and all at once I could see the way to find the answer."

"Dear me. You must have worried about that all night. Well, what's the secret? Are you going to tell me?"

"You start with the hour hand. That wheel turns around twice every twenty-four hours. You count the cogs on it, and the wheel next to it, and divide one into the other. Then you go on to the next wheel. Do you see?"

"Maybe. In a way. It looks like you will have a few cogs left over. But you can divide and multiply, even so. Do you remember what I told you about division?"

But David had already started. While Mrs. Carder cooked their porridge, he counted cogs again, scratched the numbers on a board with a piece of charcoal, and began the painful process of division. She put their plates on the edge of the hearth while she came over to watch, and a long hour passed before they were through and David could point to each wheel and tell her the answer, how many times it turned in twenty-four hours.

She sighed with relief, picked up his bowl and handed it to him. "I'm glad that's over. Now maybe we can get on with other things, like eating. I'm starved. And the food is cold."

They didn't mind, though. After breakfast, David put the wheels in place, and cleaned the inside of the clock

59

case. Before he put the movement back, and the weights, he lifted the walnut box.

"This is still heavy," he said. "There's nothing in it, no weights, and it's still heavy. I wonder why."

Carefully he put the works in, pushing the little pegs that held it in place, hung the pendulum, passed the strings over the pulleys, hung the weights, and wound them up. Then the face, and the hands.

He looked up at Mrs. Carder.

"Are you ready? I'm going to start it."

She nodded. "Go ahead, son."

He gave the pendulum a little push. It swung back and forth. It ticked once, went slower and slower, gradually stopped with a little wobble. He frowned, gave it another shove, so hard that it banged on the case. Again there was a feeble tick, the brass bob went from side to side, slowed until it was barely moving, and stopped. David glared at it. His mother said not a word. For a long minute he looked at it. Then he shut the door of the case, picked up the clock, carried it to the mantel and set it there. He turned around, and stalked across the room.

"David."

"Yes'm." He stopped in front of the door.

"You didn't finish the job. It isn't running."

"No. It won't run. I can't make it go."

"You mean you're giving up. Is that it?"

He didn't answer.

"David, you remember how it was with the fence. And you remember the story Sam Skookum told you, about the first Indian and the log. Maybe there was a lesson in that. Something about being patient. Or stubborn."

"Mom—I'm tired of looking at wheels and counting cogs. It's too complicated. I can't do it."

She said nothing for a moment. "All right, boy," she said finally. "I understand." She turned back to her work.

David went out the door, shut it harder than he usually did, marched to the chopping block and gripped the handle of the ax. He glowered at the sticks waiting to be chopped, at the broken board in the barn door, at the green woods around the cabin. He stared down at a long fir chunk that was to be cut up when he got around to it. He pushed some of the sticks out of the way, swung the ax around in a great arc and delivered a furious chop at the log. The blade bit deep, and he wrenched it loose, brought it down again and again, as hard as he could.

He chopped and chopped until he had cut all the way through it. He stopped to wipe his sleeve across his face, and rub his hands on his trousers. He was panting, and when he clamped his lips shut, his breath came noisily through his nose. He started swinging the ax again, at the center of the wood. The ax went more slowly, but it kept going up and down, chunk, chunk, chunk, chips flying, until there was another cut all the way through.

Even then he didn't stop. He swung and hammered and struck at the pieces until all the wood was split into firewood and the dogtrot was littered from end to end with chips and sticks. He gave one last swing, brought the ax firmly down into the chopping block, and he sat on the block, rested his arm on the handle and looked at what he had done. Finally he got up slowly, stooped and picked up the pieces, threw them into a pile. He found that by arranging them carefully he could build the pile high and straight. It took some study, but at last he was done, and he imagined that the pile was the battlement of a castle, carefully disguised to look like a pile of firewood. He felt better. He had taken care of the log. He glanced over to

61

the fence. He had built a good fence, too. With help. He wondered. Maybe there was something he was learning, after all. Maybe there was something important about figuring out problems when he came to them. Like making the clock run, for instance.

The clock. He yanked the ax out of the chopping block, whirled it down in a great chop that almost split the block in two, and jarred it so hard that the castle of firewood toppled, great timbers crashed about the ears of the defenders, and valiant knights fell headlong into the moat, silently, without a complaint. He stared down at the ruin, and frowned darkly.

"Die, dogs!" he whispered. He sighed. It was time to milk Rosy.

Two days later, the sun came out bright and warm in the morning and they decided to have a look at the field. Maybe it was about time to plant, and though they had no way to plow, they felt that they should see about it anyway.

Together they set out, after leaving Rosy munching happily in her favorite spot. They had to cross the creek, just above the beaver's home, and when they came through the trees and stood on the bank, Mrs. Carder pointed with her hand.

"David. What did I tell you?"

"The dam!"

He could hardly believe it. It was in place again, as though it had been there all the time. There was a difference, true enough. The sticks were new, and the chewed ends were a clean white. It was even a little higher than it used to be. And stretching back from it was the pond, wider and bigger than ever.

"Now, Mr. David Carder, what do you say about that? What do you think about your little friend?"

David had nothing to say. He shook his head and studied the neat way the dam was put together. It looked as though it would never wash out again.

They went on to the field, saw that there was some clearing to do where a tree had fallen. They felt of the ground. It was beginning to dry. It was almost time to begin plowing.

Mrs. Carder looked across the field. "When your father left, he said he'd probably be back in time to plant. If he wasn't, he said we should ask Martin for help."

"Martin's gone."

"Yes, son. There's nobody we can turn to. Except the neighbors."

"The Griffins?"

She nodded. "Maybe I'll have to humble myself, and ask for help."

"You couldn't do that, Mom. It would be saying you'd done the wrong thing, and you know that isn't so."

"Well, I guess I can do some growing up, too. Forgiving is better than holding a grudge. And I'd say that even if we did have our own horse."

They roamed around the field, talking about what there was to do. When they got back to the cabin, Mrs. Carder went inside and David stayed in the open, watching the way the trees were leafing out and everything was getting greener. After a bit he turned toward the barn, pulled the door open and went to the far wall. He thought he had better make sure the sacks of seed were still in good condition.

He whipped off the tarpaulin.

His eyes opened wide. The sacks were gone.

A few sticks had been put in their place, enough to hold the tarpaulin up. But the sacks were no longer there.

He went to the cabin door, told his mother. She came out, and the two of them stared at the empty space along the wall. They looked all around, over and under everything. There was no doubt at all about it.

"Mom. Somebody stole it. Somebody carried all those sacks away. At night. Or when we were busy inside."

"It's hard to explain, son. Not many people knew about our seed. It was hidden."

David thought. "Dan Griffin knew. And Mr. Griffin. And Martin. Nobody else, except us, and Dad. And—Sam. You know what I think?"

"Be careful, boy. Try to think straight, now."

"I know who did it. Dan Griffin. He took them."

Mrs. Carder folded her arms. "Maybe it seems like he did. Maybe we can't see it any other way. But maybe we're wrong. We don't know that he did, now, do we?"

David's eyes narrowed and his jaw tightened. "He's the only one who would."

"I guess you didn't hear me right, boy. I said you have to be sure. You have to be mighty sure, at a time like this. Now you just quiet down and think. What if you accused Dan of stealing it, and then you discovered it wasn't so? What would you do then?"

"Mom. It's gone. Isn't that plain enough?"

"No. It's not. We still don't know what happened to it."

In the cabin they sat down at the table across from each other. Mrs. Carder put her hands in front of her, began tapping her fingers.

"Well," she said. "What can we do now?"

"Mom, I don't know. Unless I get more supplies from Mr. Dickins."

She shook her head. "No. We already owe him for the other supplies. It wouldn't be right to ask him. He's having a struggle too, son. Lots of people owe him money. He's a little too generous for his own good." She sighed. "Maybe we better add things up and see just where we stand. That the way you look at it, son?"

"Yes, Mom."

"Let's see—we lost one horse and a gun, but we have Mr. Cox's gun now. We have a cow, enough milk and butter. No flour or bacon, but plenty of venison. You shot a mountain lion and got a new coat. And you built a fence. But we don't have any seed. Or a way to plow." She glanced around the room. "We still have a good place to live. And a clock that won't run. We've done everything we could. Now I guess we'll have to ask for help. And I hate to do that."

David stared at the mantel. "There's one more thing we can do, Mom."

"Yes? What, son?"

"The clock. I think I can fix it now. Even if it won't make much difference."

"I thought you gave it up."

"I did. Now it's the last thing I can do anything about."

"Hmm." She tapped the ends of her fingers again. "You mean we're not quite through yet. That there's one more thing we can do for ourselves."

"Yes."

"Well, you go ahead. And then we'll see. Maybe somehow things will look different with a clock ticking. We'll see."

He took the clock down, set it on the table, opened the door and removed the hands and the face. He had been thinking about the way it worked. He swung the pendulum, studied the way the little curved piece at the top rocked back and forth and the sharp ends moved in and out of the escapement wheel. The wheel pushed against the piece with each swing of the rod. But the curved piece never quite let the cogs pass. Maybe it was so worn that it was too low.

A short wooden lever held the axle of the curved piece. If it were moved up just a little, just enough to raise it— he shoved it gently, gave the pendulum another push. All at once the clock went Tock, Tock, Tock, the escapement clicked around, and the verge moved in and out.

"David! It's running!"

He grinned. It was, sure enough. He watched it go, watched the pendulum rock from one side to the other, the light glinting on the brass bob. He put the face back on, pressed the hands in place, lifted the clock onto the mantel. There he started it again, set the hands a little before three o'clock just because that seemed right, shut the door, and stepped back.

The long hand moved slowly toward three. There was a whirring noise. Minutes passed. Then another whirring, and after that came a gentle bong, bong, bong, as the clock struck.

It made all the difference in the world. The friendly tock-tocking and the musical chiming floated around the room, and the cabin seemed warmer and happier. Mrs. Carder began to hum softly, and it was nicer in the cabin than it had been for a long time.

"David."

"Yes?"

"Hasn't been any music in this house for weeks."

"No."

"No violin music. Why did you stop practicing, son?"

"Don't you remember? It sounded awful. Dad used to leave the cabin when I screeched on it."

"Seems to me your trouble was that you couldn't keep time. Wasn't that it?"

"Yes, Mom. Partly. Why?"

She went over to where the violin was hanging in the shadows beside the fireplace, took it and the bow off the hook, tightened the frog, stuck the violin under her chin and tuned it. She handed it to David.

"Here, boy. Now you won't have any more trouble keeping time."

"Why not?"

She held up a finger, wagged it in time with the ticking of the old clock. "That's why. You have a metronome. Something to beat time for you."

David pressed his lips together. He took the violin, got it in position, dragged the bow heavily over the strings, one drag to a tick, up, down, squawk, squawk.

Mrs. Carder touched his elbow, and he stopped. "Son, not quite like that—"

"Mom, I've forgotten all the tunes. You play it now. You haven't played it in a long time. Not since Dad left."

"Well, maybe I will. Just for the sake of old times." She put the violin under her chin, drew the bow across the strings, began to play. It was an old song, one David remembered from long ago, and it floated sweetly around the room.

Suddenly a strange thing happened. They both turned their heads toward the mantel. Toward the clock. For the clock had begun to strike again, and when it struck four times, it did not stop. Five, six, on up to twelve—and still it went on, bong, bong, bong. They counted with it until it reached seventy-five. There was a click, and it stopped.

"Well, now," said Mrs. Carder, hanging up the fiddle, "what would make it act like that?"

David thought. "There's a little wire that comes down each time it rings. It has to be bent just so. Or maybe something got stuck. I better look at it."

He lifted the clock down, carried it to the table. He opened the door, removed the hands and face again, wound up the chiming side and let it strike. This time it struck only five times. He tried it again. Six. Just like it was supposed to do.

"That makes two things I don't understand about this clock."

"What's that, Davy?"

"Why it should ring so many times, and why it is so heavy. It doesn't make sense for a plain box to be as heavy as that, even with the weights."

He laid the case flat on the table, studied it carefully all around. He hadn't put it down like this before. He hadn't seen the bottom of the case before. Now he saw it for the first time, and the little wooden door in it, a small square piece on tiny hinges with a flat brass latch.

Mrs. Carder leaned over his shoulder and stared at it with him. "What on earth is that for, boy? What does that little latch do?"

Slowly David pushed the brass fastener aside.

Immediately the door flew open. A round piece of metal rolled out and clinked to the table. And another. And many more after it.

"I do declare, son!"

"Mom, look!"

"I never—why, no wonder that clock was so heavy. And there must be more in there."

70

She picked up one of them and studied it. David did the same.

"They're coins, Mom, pennies and things like that. Some of them are so worn I can't even see what they are. And look—this one is an old dollar." He held it close. "It says Liberty at the top, and 1804 at the bottom. But all those pennies—look at them!"

Mrs. Carder shook her head. "So that's what your grandfather tried to tell me. He had been using the old clock for a coin bank. No wonder. How much do you suppose there is?"

"We'll count them, Mom." And they did. They stacked the coins, little and big, and added them slowly. It took a long time. And when they were through, it was quite a bit.

"Ten dollars and eleven cents," said David. "Or about that."

"Hmm." She looked at him, and he stared back. "Are you thinking the same thing I am, son?"

"Yes. We can buy something with it."

"Flour?"

He shook his head.

"Food?"

He shook his head again. She smiled.

"Seed, Davy?"

He nodded. "Yes. There's enough for two sacks, I think."

"But not enough money for a horse."

"No, but enough for seed. When we have that, maybe we can borrow a horse somewhere, or something will show up. Or Dad will come back."

"It's like what the beaver did, in a way, isn't it?"

He nodded. "Yes, Mom. Like we should figure it was going to work out right."

She turned her head and stared toward the window. "I don't know how you'll get the sacks home. But maybe all we have to worry about is doing one thing at a time. Things look different now, don't they? You can go down to Oregon City and see what you can do about it. But— there's one thing I'm going to take care of first, before we do anything else."

"What's that?"

"I'm going to patch things up with our neighbors. I'm going to send Mrs. Griffin a berry pie. I've kept a little smidgin of flour just in case we ran out of everything else. I'll use that, and the last crock of berries. But it doesn't matter. It's hard for folks to be nice after they've had words. I'll make the first move. You can take them the pie as soon as I make it, tomorrow morning."

"Mom—you aren't doing this just so we can ask them to help us?"

She smiled. "No, son. I'm just doing it because we have to be on good terms with the neighbors if we stay here. And I have a feeling we're going to be here a good long time, son."

Chapter 5

Betsy

THE NEXT morning he set out for the Griffin place.
In his left hand, hanging in a knotted cloth, was a berry pie. In the other hand was the gun. It was a fine, warm, spring day. As he stood on the other side of the open area, he turned, waved to his mother, and went on into the deep woods.

The great trees rose above, and he lifted his head, heard a bird singing. Beyond the woods, the path curved down a little valley, not far from where Scat Creek spread out noisily in a long series of rapids just above several deep, quiet pools. Before many days had passed, he was going to come down here with his pole and spend a long afternoon doing nothing but fish. It gave him little chills of excitement to think how the trout would snag onto his hook and tug.

He stayed on the path, switched the gun and the pie to

rest his arms, and plodded along steadily, on through the groves that lay past the forest, on down the valley, while the sun slowly moved across the cloudless sky.

He came at last to the spot where he could see the Griffins' farm. It was set against the hill, a cabin and a barn, and their fields were off to the left, where the land sloped. There was a horse in the middle of the field, and two figures by it. He frowned. He didn't know what he would say to them when they met. It was going to be hard to keep from saying what was in his mind. His mother had given him instructions about that. He hoped he could follow them.

As he came along the edge of the field, the man and the boy saw him. They didn't wave. Dan left his father and came slouching across toward David.

Dan waited in the path while David came to him.

"You're trespassing," said Dan.

"I'm what?"

"You're on our property. Seems to me you Carders should know enough to stay away from here."

"I'm on the path," said David. "Anybody has a right to walk on the path."

"What did you come down here for, anyway?"

"My mother sent a pie. A berry pie."

Dan sneered. "To make up for the one the Indian stole, I suppose. Or maybe you folks figure you need help now, and you'll try to be friendly. Is that it?"

David remembered what his mother had said. He was to deliver the pie, and be a gentleman, and say nothing about other matters. He remembered, but it didn't do any good. He felt his cheeks grow hot.

"We're not beholden to you folks," he said. "And we

74

don't aim to be. We're not asking for anything, not even what belongs to us."

Dan hunched his head. "What do you mean by that?"

"I mean some sacks of seed."

Dan's eyes widened, and he glanced over his shoulder. He smiled, stuck his hands in his pockets. "Why don't you ask your Indian friend about it? He's the one that stole your three sacks."

David nodded. "I guess it was you, after all. I didn't say somebody stole three sacks. How did you know?"

Dan flared up, waved his fists suddenly in front of his face.

"I don't know anything about it, Dave Carder. All I know is you better turn around right now and get back to your farm. I'll count to five. When I'm through counting, you better be on your way. You hear me? One!"

David looked at him. He heard him count, one, two, three—He moved aside, put down the gun, took off his coat, and removed the cloth from the pie. He took it carefully, holding it in his hand.

"I was told to bring this pie, and I'm bringing it, Dan Griffin. You better get out of the way or I'll walk right over you. I'm coming whether you have brains enough to count to five or not. Out of my road, Dan!"

"Five!" Dan put his hands on his hips, spread his legs wide and stood there. David took one step, then another, until he was only a few feet away.

"Here you are!" said David.

He lifted the pie and pushed it squarely in Dan's face. It was hard to say what happened after that. There was a yelp of amazement, two figures started swinging their arms, hammering and punching back and forth, and it was soon impossible to tell one face from the other. Both were stained red from the pie.

One of them fell backwards, and the other came down on top of him. They rolled sideways, wrestling and flailing, pulling and hauling and grunting.

"Here, here!" said a voice out of the air above them. They both sat up, blinked their eyes at the man looming over them. It was Mr. Griffin.

"What are you trying to do? Kill each other? Your faces—they're all bloody! And your hands—you're both bleeding!"

Dan wiped a sleeve across his face.

"It's pie, Paw," he said.

"Pie?"

"Berry pie."

"How did a berry pie get tangled up in this?"

"I brought it," said David. "From my mother. She said to give it to Mrs. Griffin. Dan wouldn't get out of the way, so—I gave it to him instead."

Mr. Griffin hrumphed and groped for words he couldn't find. Finally he poked Dan with the toe of his boot.

"Get up, you two. Get up and go to the cabin. We'll get to the bottom of this when you wash your faces. Now move."

David picked up his coat and his gun and the three of them walked slowly up the slope to the cabin. When they reached it, the door opened and Mrs. Griffin stood there.

"For heaven's sake!"

"It's all right. It's only berry pie. The boys were fighting over it, and it got smeared around a little. Go on in, you two, and wash at the basin in the corner."

When they had cleaned their faces and stood in front of the fireplace, Mr. and Mrs. Griffin confronted them. The whole story came out—or most of it. Nobody mentioned the stolen sacks.

"Why did your mother send us a pie, boy?"

Mrs. Griffin folded her arms. "Now, Paw, you settle down. If Mrs. Carder wants to be neighborly and send us a pie, she doesn't need any reasons."

"Well. It wasn't you she chased off her place and threatened with a gun."

"Never mind. You have a short temper, Paw. You flared up too fast when that Indian boy came through here, and you probably gave Mrs. Carder good cause to treat you like she did. Now maybe you can have the good manners to forgive and forget." She turned to David. "You tell your mother we thank her for the pie, even if it didn't get to us in very good shape. I think it was very nice of her, and we appreciate it. You tell her that, won't you?"

David nodded. "Yes'm."

She reached toward the mantel, took down a letter and held it out. "Here's something else. This came a few days ago. I was just about ready to bring it up to you people myself. I couldn't get either of these two to take it. They were too stubborn. I'm ashamed of them."

David took the letter. He recognized his father's handwriting.

"Ma'am," he said, "I expect I'd better get this to my mother right away. She'll be anxious to see it. I'd best be on my way."

Mr. Griffin moved forward half a step. "Boy—maybe things haven't gone like they should between us. Maybe I have been a little hasty now and then. You tell your mother that, too. I don't aim to be unfriendly."

"Yes, sir."

"We're not bad neighbors. Even Dan here isn't such a

77

bad fellow." He put an arm awkwardly around Dan's shoulders. "He's ambitious, I'll have to say that. He's planning on sowing another field to grain next week. I don't know where he figures on getting the seed, but he says he has plans."

Dan's face turned a fiery red, and he looked away.

"I'd best go," said David. "I'll tell Mom what you said."

He ran almost all the way back to the farm, the letter snug in his shirt pocket, the coat and the gun in his hands. He ran until he was out of breath and had to stop to rest.

When he finally came through the big woods and into the clearing, he was walking slowly. He heard the sound of an ax coming from the field. It was a regular chopping, not the way his mother chopped, but big strokes. He moved on past the cabin, across the creek, over to the side of the field where the tree was down. There he saw two figures. One was his mother, and the other, swinging the ax, was Sam.

He sauntered toward them.

"Well," he said. "Look who's back. Sam Skookum. I thought you got lost in the woods."

Sam turned around with a grin and pushed his hair out of his sweaty face. "Hello. It wouldn't make much difference if I did get lost. I'd still be home."

"Sam came along about an hour ago," said Mrs. Carder. "He found me out here trying to gnaw the tree in two, and he offered to help. He's got that tree chopped into pieces small enough to carry away now." She looked at David's shirt. "You have an accident, boy? What's that red all over you?"

David looked down at it. "Berry pie. Dan wasn't going to let me by, so I delivered the pie right there."

"Hmm. Fine way to treat a pie I'd slaved over. Doesn't

sound like you two got along very well. What's that sticking out of your pocket?"

He handed her the letter, and explained how it had been sitting on the Griffins' mantel. Hurriedly she opened the page and began to read to herself. David watched her, and Sam turned to chop off the last big branch.

"What's it say, Mom? Is he coming back before long?"

She paid no attention to him for several minutes, reading slowly and carefully, a smile on her face. Then she looked at him.

"He doesn't know for sure, son. It all depends on how things go. Maybe he'll be back in a week, or two weeks."

"Did the people get down river all right?"

"Yes. It was hard work for all of them. Mostly he had trouble just keeping warm, and fed. I'll let you read it by yourself later." She looked at the last lines again. "He's worried about how we're getting along. He told us to move in with the Griffins, or go down to Oregon City and stay with Mr. and Mrs. Dickins." She smiled at him again, and there was nothing they had to say about that.

In a few minutes all three of them got behind a section of the tree, pried and pushed until they rolled it into the brush, and they picked up the branches, cleaned off the ground, and walked back to the cabin.

While Mrs. Carder got dinner, Sam and David brought in more firewood, and sat down at the table.

"Sam's on his way back to the mission school," said Mrs. Carder.

"School!" said David. "I thought you'd had enough school for a while."

Sam grunted. "The chief got mad," he said. "When he saw me coming down the beach he chased me for a whole mile, until both of us got out of breath and sat down. He was more out of breath than I was, but I was tired. Well, he said he was going to give me the biggest, hardest whipping I had ever gotten in my life, but he wasn't quite ready to start on it. It reminded him of a story. When he got through with his story he grumbled at me and then he told me I had to go back to the mission school. He gave himself enough time to think it over, I guess, and he decided it wouldn't do any good to beat me. So he said I had to go back. And here I am on my way back."

"Sam," said Mrs. Carder, "do you want company tomorrow? All the way to town?"

"Yes. I do. You and David?"

"No. Just David. We still have a place to watch after. Besides, Mr. Carder might come back. David will go with you. How does that sound to you, David?"

And so it was that the next morning, early, before the sun was up, and while the dew was still heavy on the ferns, and heavy spider webs strung across the path, David and Sam Skookum set out for Oregon City.

In David's pocket was a heavy bag of coins. In the crook of his arm was the gun. And on his back was the mountain lion coat.

They made good time. Sam showed him the trick of jogging along in a slow run, lifting his feet no higher than need be, and stopping only when they had to.

The sun was coming up over the far mountains when they came to the Griffin place. Sam stopped, and David noticed for the first time that Sam was carrying a small bundle tied with a thong.

Sam held it up. "You wait a minute. I'm going to pay for that apple pie."

David stood there while Sam walked to the door of the

cabin and knocked. It opened a crack, then wider, and the amazed face of Mr. Griffin stuck out.

"You!" he said.

Sam shoved the bundle at him. "Here," he said. "I brought you this. It's for the pie."

The man took it, looked at it, and raised his head. Sam was already walking away. "Wait a minute, young fellow. What's this all about?"

Sam went over to David, and together they started running. Just before they passed over the brow of the hill, David looked back. He could see Mr. Griffin standing at the corner of his house, watching them.

"I guess it's not any of my business, Sam. But what did you give him?"

"An animal pelt. Enough to buy two thousand pies."

From then on it was jog, jog, on and on, over one little hill after another, down rolling draws, across stretches where the trees were widely scattered and the grass hissed around their feet.

After they stopped for lunch, David tied the sleeves of his coat so it would hang down his back. Sam was impatient to be on his way again, and David had to hurry to keep up. The bag of coins in his pocket kept banging against his leg. Several times he considered whether he should cache the gun and the coat behind a tree somewhere, but he knew he shouldn't.

They passed a cabin and waved to people as they passed. A man trotted by on horseback and stopped for a few words. Not long after noon, they came over a rise and saw the great valley below them—the sloping hills, the clusters of trees, the black forests beyond rising to a snowy peak, and the river winding into sight here and there.

When they came down the road to the edge of the water they had to wait for the ferryman. Sam had brought some corn cakes and jerked meat, and the two of them munched while the man rowed his boat over to them. Again the man charged them nothing, but said he would collect on the return trip.

They came into town soon afterwards, and stared around them at the houses. There was a fine odor of smoke in the air, and it seemed to David that there were more people. He wondered how it would be to live in a city.

"Well," said Sam, "I guess this is where we part company. You come to my village before the middle of summer. There's a shipwreck down the beach we can investigate. And a cave. And we can go fishing."

"And there's the chief, Sam. I'd like to hear him tell one of his stories. Do you think I could learn enough Chinook to understand him?"

"It would be easy. When the chief tells a story he waves his arms in the air and trots back and forth and puffs and blows and flips his elbows like wings—you can understand the story just by watching him, almost. You'll have to see for yourself." He put out his hand, and they shook hands. "I still have a way to go, Dave. Don't forget now —you're coming to my village." And then he was gone.

David turned and walked down the street, toward Mr. Dickins' store.

There was nobody near him in the street, or hardly anybody. Only himself and an Indian that was riding toward him.

He moved aside so he would be out of the way, and watched idly as the horse came up to him and started by.

"Hey!" he yelled suddenly.

The Indian drew on the reins, stopped the horse, and turned to stare at David. His face was expressionless.

"That horse—that's Betsy! That's my horse!"

He ran around her, looked for the scar on her neck. The Indian's hand was resting against her mane, and the blanket coat he wore hung over the mark. David reached out, quickly lifted the blanket.

"There!" He pointed at the scar. "It is Betsy. I knew it was. Do you understand? My—horse!"

The Indian gazed back stolidly. Then he straightened up, pounded on his chest with his fist. "Kloash Kuitan!" he said. "My horse!" At almost the same moment, he prodded Betsy and she began to amble forward, while David stood there in the street, watching them go.

But this time he wouldn't let the animal out of his sight, whether she had an Indian in her saddle or not. This time he was going to follow her. He was going to get her back.

"Stop!" shouted David. "You stop!" And he began to run after her.

She didn't stop. The Indian didn't even turn his head to look around. All the Indian did was to rock slowly from side to side, hunch down in his blanket, and ride right down the middle of the road that wound along the edge of the river out of town.

David hung the gun in the crook of his elbow, held a hand under the pocket full of coins so it wouldn't keep swinging against his leg, and trotted as fast as she did. He didn't know how long he would have to chase her. He didn't know quite what he would do when he got there, wherever it was they were going. He was just certain he was going to do everything he could to get her back. He had stopped hoping he would ever see her again some time ago—and there she was, trotting ahead of him down the road.

"Betsy!" he called. He knew it was no use to yell. It only used up his strength. He set his lips, plodded grimly on, his coat feeling very hot and heavy.

It went on like that for an hour. And then suddenly they came to a curve in the road, wound around a thick grove of trees, and right ahead was an Indian village of several teepees and rounded huts. Many Indians were walking back and forth, dogs were barking, and children were yelling.

The Indian on the horse stopped, rose up and called out in a loud voice. David couldn't understand a word. Several times the man said the same thing. Other Indians stopped to listen and look. Slowly they walked toward David, and formed a tight circle around him.

David looked from one face to another. He couldn't tell what was on their minds. He pointed to Betsy, and tapped his own chest. "That's my horse," he said. "She ran away. Now I have found her. You see? That's my horse—I want her back."

One of the Indians, a tall, wiry brave with a buckskin shirt, stepped forward and looked at David. In one swift motion, he grasped David's gun, twisted it out of his grasp, and shoved him backwards.

David stumbled, but quickly got up again. The brave began to talk, pointing at Betsy and her rider, making motions with his hands, his voice growing louder and louder. Even David could begin to see what he meant—that Betsy belonged to the Indian, and that David was trying to take something that was not his.

Somebody shoved him, hard. He tottered over against

the other side of the circle of natives. Hands reached up and shoved him back, spinning him around, bouncing him from side to side like a toy. They started to laugh, to point their fingers at him, and howl with glee. He was sure it wouldn't be long before the coins bounced right out of his pocket.

For some reason, they suddenly stopped. It became very quiet. David steadied himself, pushed his hair out of his eyes. He stared around him. The Indians drew back a little, and made room for a short, but very dignified, old Indian who strode into their midst and said only a few words.

He turned toward David, scowling. "What's going on here?" he growled.

David pointed at Betsy. "That's my animal. She ran away a few weeks ago, and now I've found her. Can I have her back, please?"

The Indian grunted. "Lucky for you I came along when I did. My people understand what you wanted. Just enough to make them good and mad. You tried to take his horse. You tried to steal it from him. Is that right?"

"She's mine. I'm not trying to steal anything."

The Indian shook his head. "She belongs to Pilchuck. She's his. He found her. I think you better go back to your town, boy, and stay out of trouble. Go now, while you can."

David glared back at the Indian. "No, I'll stay here until you give her to me. Listen—I can prove she's mine." He pointed to the scar. "See that? A mountain lion clawed her there."

The chief ran his fingers over the scar and grunted. "Could have been a mountain lion, or something else. Not much proof. Just a mark on her."

85

David looked down at the side of his coat. At the paw that was dangling there, the paw of the mountain lion. He lifted it, held it toward the Indian.

"That's the claw right there," he said. "Doesn't that prove it?"

"Hmm. Take off the coat."

David shrugged out of it, handed it to the Indian. The man held the paw up to the scar while others crowded around him. Carefully he pressed on it. The claws spread out. They matched the three long marks. David held his breath while the Indian turned toward him again.

There was a smile on the man's face. "Maybe so," he said. "Maybe it was that very paw." He handed him his coat, and David pulled it on. "I think it was that paw, boy. You look honest to me, anyway. I think you're right. I think that's your horse."

He turned around, spoke quickly and sharply to the Indian who had ridden in on Betsy. The fellow waved his hands, talked as though he were explaining something, but he got nowhere. Finally he shrugged his shoulders and walked away. The chief put the reins in David's hand.

"There. Now you have your horse. Maybe you learned something about Indians, too. Maybe you found out they aren't so bad after all."

"I only know two Indians," said David, "and they're both good. You, and Sam Skookum."

The chief laughed suddenly, his eyes turning to small bright spots in the wrinkles of his skin. "You know Sam Skookum? Do you know his father, the chief?"

"No."

"When you do, you will know three good Indians. Or two good ones and one very funny Indian. He tells long stories. Crazy stories. I could listen to him a long time."

The Indian who had been on Betsy came back, handed a rifle to the chief. "Here, boy," said the chief, and gave it to David. "This was with the horse. There were some supplies, too, but they were gone a long time ago. Maybe you owed us that for taking care of your horse."

David held out his hand. The chief shook it, and slapped him on the shoulder. "Now climb up there and go, boy. You have your horse and your gun. And when you see Chief Skookum, tell him about us."

When David arrived at the Dickins' house, it was almost supper time. He took care of Betsy, talked to her and rubbed the white spot on her muzzle, and let her rub her head against him. He put her in the barn behind the house for the night.

And when he stretched out in bed to go to sleep that night, he felt good. He had reason to feel good. Several reasons. Somehow, things were slowly getting straightened out again, one by one.

Chapter 6

Pioneer Engineer

THE NEXT morning was full of surprises, mostly for Mr. Dickins. He was a pleasant man, full of laughs and jokes, and he took David into the store long before it was time to get up. It still felt like the middle of the night.

He lit a candle on the counter, scratched his chin, and frowned and mumbled to himself as he began to assemble the supplies. He brought one sack of seed and a small paper bag of vegetable seeds, and set them on the floor.

David looked at the one big sack and the one little sack. "I guess we'll need more than that, sir," he said. "I think we'll need at least two big sacks."

Mr. Dickins bobbed his head. "I know, son. And I'm going to do what I can for your folks. I'll give you what I can. But I don't see how I can give you more than this."

"You mean there isn't any more seed?"

The man spread his hands. "There's plenty of it. But these are hard times for me. Everybody is doing business on credit. They promise to pay with wheat—when they can harvest. I can barely manage to keep this store going. You're welcome to this much."

"Oh," said David. He dug down in his pocket, brought out the heavy bag. "I 'spect you didn't understand, Mr. Dickins. I forgot to tell you about this." He undid the string, held up the bag and let the coins come rolling and clinking into a heap on the counter.

Mr. Dickins leaned forward with a gasp. He picked up one of the coins, held it close to the flame while he inspected it carefully. He chuckled. "That's hard money, all right. Take me an hour to count it. What does it come to, son?"

"Ten dollars. About that. Will it be enough?"

Mr. Dickins laughed. "Yes, it will. Indeed yes. Enough to pay for your other supplies, too. I'll get you everything you want."

It was soon ready. Mr. Dickins tied three sacks of seed behind the saddle; and a big package of garden seed, and a paper box that he said was for David's mother.

The sun was just coming up when David climbed onto Betsy and took the reins.

"Just a minute, boy." Mr. Dickins gave him the 1804 dollar, and several small coins. "You'll likely want to keep this cartwheel for a souvenir, and you'll need the rest to get across the river. This should do it. I'll see Mr. Cox one of these days, and I'll give him the rifle that he loaned you." He leaned forward and gave David a hard pat on the leg. "Now say hello to your mother, boy, and stick to the road. Good luck!"

David clucked to Betsy, flapped the reins, and she

started down the street so swiftly that David just had time to turn and wave before they were around the corner.

"Gee-up, girl!" He was on his way, and it felt good. He took a deep breath of cold, clean air, and smiled. Betsy had a big load, but she seemed happy to be with David again.

When he came to the slope of the river bank and stopped for the ferry, the man was sitting there on the edge of a canoe. He came up and looked at Betsy and her burden.

"Going across, son?"

"I'd like to."

"I'll get the flat. I'm afraid I'll have to charge you something. Can you spare some powder or bullets?"

David dug the small coins out of his pocket. "Will this do?"

"Well. Indeed it will. It's nice to find somebody that pays with money nowadays." He picked the coins out of David's palm. "You just wait there, mister, and I'll be back."

The flat boat was brought around to the little slip; David got down and led Betsy forward by the bridle and tied her to a post. They started out. The man pushed at the rear of the boat with a pole until they were well out from shore and drifting downstream before he took hold of two long oars and stood up as he leaned against them, and the boat moved slowly across.

In the afternoon he rode past the Griffins. He could see them out in the field, turning to wave at him and stare. He waved back, flipped the reins and kept going. When he moved up the far slope, he looked toward them. They were still watching. He wondered how Dan was coming with his field.

The ride through the big woods, where the brush had grown on both sides, was noisy. The bushes whipped and snapped against Betsy's sides, and David stopped her several times, got down, and rubbed her muzzle and talked to her. It was good to have her again.

When they came to the clearing, close enough to see the cabin, David paused for a moment. A figure came out and stood waiting. David sat up straight, clucked to the horse, and Betsy arched her neck, trotted across the clearing and up to the dogtrot as though she had just started the journey.

Mrs. Carder came forward as David slid to the ground. She stared at him, at the horse, at the sacks tied behind the saddle.

"Betsy! It's Betsy!" And she put an arm around her neck, rubbed her muzzle fondly. "You brought her back, David. You found her. Welcome home, girl!" She turned toward David. "How did it happen, son? Where was she?"

"Mom, it's a long story. It will take time. Before we do anything else, let's get the things off her back. There's a package for you, something Mr. Dickins sent. You go open it inside. Then we can talk."

Supper was late that night. Mrs. Carder didn't get it ready until she had gone through the box and examined the buttons, cloth, ribbons, spools of thread, packets of needles, all the things she had wanted for a long time. And David had to take care of the animals before he came in and sat down at the table.

All during supper Mrs. Carder kept silent and watched

91

until David ate the last bite and pushed his plate away.

"Now, boy," she said. "Now you can talk. Tell me everything that happened." And he did. She had questions, many of them, about the town, the people he had seen. Finally he yawned and shook his head.

"I don't think there's any more to tell, Mom. Not tonight."

She patted his hand. "All right, son. I'll save the rest of my questions until tomorrow. But I do want to tell you one thing more. I'm proud of you, son."

After they poked the fire together, David crawled into his bed. He lay awake for a while, watching the light flicker above, and listening to the slow tick of the clock. It was good to be home. And to think about what had happened.

The next day they got to work early. It was four days before they had the field plowed, seeded, and dragged with the harrow. Four long days that David and his mother took turns going back and forth behind the balky wooden plow while Betsy tugged it patiently, and then walked up and down with sacks slung over their shoulders, throwing the seed out with a sweep of the hand.

After that, there was the vegetable garden. It took almost as long. But eventually it was done, and there were long, neat rows in the freshly planted ground, with the fence around it. It was in the hot afternoon when they sat down on a log in the shade beside the cabin and gazed at what they had accomplished. It was beautiful. The birds were singing, Betsy and Rosy were browsing in the grass. The work was all done.

"David."

"Yes'm?"

"I don't expect we can soldier on the job now."

"Ma'am?"

"We'll need rain for the garden. The field will be all right, but vegetables are different. We'll have to have rain, or we'll have to get water to the garden some other way."

"We'll get rain. There will be plenty of that. Remember how it came down that night?"

"Yes, son, I do. But you can't count on it. I've been puzzling this out. Now there's plenty of water in the creek. The only trouble is, it's over there, and the garden's over here. Maybe we'll have to carry it. In the keg."

David whistled. "It's heavy, Mom."

She nodded. "I know. Let's hope we have enough rain to see us through."

David looked across the long garden, across to the alders growing along the creek. It would be a hard task.

A little later a strange thing happened. There was the sound of voices carrying over the clearing, a whap! whap! and a yell, and then one deep voice.

David and Mrs. Carder got up and looked toward the shadows beneath the trees. At first they saw nothing. One of the shadows moved, slouched into the sunshine, walked slowly around the garden toward them.

They didn't know for sure who it was until the straw hat lifted a little. It was Dan Griffin. He paused, looked back at the woods, jammed his hands far down in his pockets, started walking again toward the cabin.

He came up to them, pulled his hat off his head and glowered.

"Mrs. Carder," he said, "it was me that did it."

David studied the boy's face, then let his gaze wander off toward the trees. It wasn't easy to look at Dan. He was blushing and having a terrible time.

"You did what, Dan?" said Mrs. Carder.

"I took it. The seed. Paw found out about it."

Mrs. Carder looked down at the ground. "I'm sorry, Dan," she said. "I reckon I know how hard it is for you to tell us, and I feel for you, boy. But I have to admire you, too, just the same."

Dan looked up. "Ma'am?"

"Even if your father drove you to it, it still took strength to come here and speak your piece. A lot of strength."

For a moment David thought Dan was going to cry, and he squirmed inside thinking about it. But Dan held himself together.

"That's not all I have to say."

"No? What else is there, Dan?"

"The crop. I sowed the field. It's all in. When I harvest, the wheat will be yours. All of it."

Another figure came toward them. It was Mr. Griffin. He moved near Dan and looked at him with a long face.

"Mrs. Carder," he said, "I guess the boy had his say."

"Yes, sir, he did."

"There's not much for me to add. We won't say we're sorry, not in so many words. We'll try to make up for it later, when harvest comes. I guess Dan told you that."

"He did."

Mr. Griffin waved a hand in the air, let it drop at his side. "We haven't exactly been good neighbors, ma'am. Seems like we caused you more grief than Indians or wild animals or anything else. Out here, in this wilderness, you'd think it would be the other way around."

Mrs. Carder nodded. "I guess that's something all of us have to come to understand. I've been a little hasty, too. I recollect I drove you off the place once. I threatened to get the gun. I've had time to think about that."

Mr. Griffin put his hands on his hips, took a deep breath, looked at Dan. "Well," he said abruptly, "we got chores to do. Come on, boy."

Without another word, the two turned, walked away from the cabin and on into the woods. David wasn't sure, but he thought Mr. Griffin put his arm around Dan's shoulders when they passed into the shadows.

"David."

"Yes, Mom?"

"You ever hear about the square of the hypotenuse?"

"The what?"

"Hmm. The square of the hypotenuse equals the sum of the squares of the other two sides. You ever come across that?"

"No, ma'am, I never did. But I don't guess it's anything I'll ever have to know about."

"Why not, son?"

"It's nothing I can use."

"Maybe you can. When you figure out how to build the new barn. How long to make it perfectly square."

"The new barn? What do we need a new barn for, Mom?"

"Why, son, there isn't room enough in the old barn for all the grain we're going to have. When we harvest our field, and Dan reaps his field, there's going to be a heap of crop to take care of. We'll need a place to put it."

David scratched the side of his head.

"Hypotenuse," he said slowly. "Hypotenuse. Seems like

every time somebody else does something for us it just means more work for me."

The next few days were clear and sunny and dry. There was no rain, not even a little drizzle.

David and his mother looked at the garden, took handfuls of the dirt, and rubbed it between their fingers.

"It's too dry, David. It needs water."

David groaned. "The keg?"

She nodded. "I don't see any other way. It will take a powerful lot of trips, too. The garden has to have water. It won't grow without it."

David went into the cabin, dragged the keg from the kitchen corner, picked it up in his arms and trudged down to the creek. It was lovely and cool there in the shadows, and he found a deeper spot where the water sluiced out between two rocks so he could hold the barrel just so and let it fill.

He balanced the keg on his shoulder, tottered back toward the cabin, holding his arm out to balance himself. He had dug little trenches down between the rows in the garden, and he tipped the keg slowly at the end of a trench, let the water pour onto the ground. A muddy pool formed and slowly trickled down a few feet. And disappeared. Soaked into the ground and vanished.

He tried the other trenches. The same thing happened. Pretty soon the keg was empty, and he made another trip to the stream. Over and over he carried the barrel to the creek, back to the garden, poured the water and watched it vanish into the ground. Each time he carried less and less, and each time he moved more slowly.

He squatted down, his elbows resting on the keg, and studied the ground. He had visions of a creek that flowed right through the dogtrot, ran into each of the trenches and watered the garden by itself. It was an idea. He jumped to his feet, ran over to the creek, waded up it until he was sure he was a little higher than the cabin. If he dug a ditch from here, the water would flow along it. He started walking through the woods. He stopped. Ahead of him was a rise in the ground.

It wouldn't work. There would be no way to get it over that spot. It was too big to dig through. He sat down again, and looked at his hands. They were red and about to blister from the rope handle. His shoulder muscles ached. Slowly he got to his feet and walked back for the keg. It looked as though there was no other way.

After one more trip, he dropped the keg by the garden, sat down beside the cabin and leaned against the logs. It wouldn't work. He couldn't do it. It was impossible. He picked up a sliver of cedar, chewed on it savagely, and spit out the splinters.

Mrs. Carder came out of the cabin and stood beside him. It was a moment before she spoke.

"If I know anything about this country, boy, I'd say we had a good chance of dry weather for two or three weeks. It's hard to tell. But it happened this way once before. I wonder if we'll have a garden."

"Why not, Mom?"

"Son, we have to have water on that piece of ground if we want a garden. The way it's going, it will just naturally dry out, and nothing will come up."

He dug his heel into the ground. "I tried, Mom. I carried that keg until I got blisters and aches. And all the water did was soak into the ground. It just disappeared. And I can't dig a ditch over here. It won't work. I just don't see how we can do anything about it."

She got down beside him, plucked a piece of grass and put it in her mouth. "I know you tried, son. I'm not blaming you for anything. It just seems a shame that we should go through everything that's happened and then finally fail, just because it won't rain. But it isn't the garden I'm thinking about, exactly. It's you."

"What do you mean by that, Mom?"

"Well, you've learned quite a bit about yourself. You've learned how to be patient, how to figure things out. Slowly, you've been growing up. And you know you're brave, son. You shot the mountain lion, and you got Betsy back."

"I was lucky," said David. "I can't take credit for that."

"All right. But you were brave just the same. Then you built the fence. You took the time to figure it out. That took some self-control."

"Sam Skookum helped me."

"I know. But you learned in the process. He showed you how to slow down and give yourself time to plan things. Then there's the clock. Of course you chopped a lot of wood before you got it going, but that was a fine thing, David. You came back to it, and you made it run. That was the best of all. I think you really grew up quite a bit when you did that. That's why I hate to see you give up on the garden. It's almost as though you could grow up so far, but no farther."

"I tried."

She stood up and smoothed her dress. "Maybe I shouldn't have said anything. But I have a feeling about it, boy, and I've had my say. I expect I won't say any more. Still, it would be nice when Jed came home if he could find everything just as it should be." She sighed.

98

"For the life of me, I don't know what you can do about it. You're a fine boy, and I'm proud of you. You should know that."

He stared over the garden and scarcely knew when she left. He had a picture in his mind, of his father coming home, walking up to the fine fence, and looking at the garden with nothing growing in it.

If he knew beaver talk, maybe he could get the beaver to help him put in a dam higher up the stream. That wouldn't work either. The water would still have to go over that small hill. The hill was higher the farther up you went.

He leaned back, thought how nice it would be if they lived on a river, where there were boats. Steamboats. He had seen the steamboat *Beaver* once, an old side-wheeler that puffed and chugged up the Columbia and the Willamette, her paddle wheels glinting in the sun as they turned.

He sat up. A flutterwheel! Just then his mother came out the doorway of the cabin and looked at him.

"Davy—what's wrong? What's that silly grin on your face for?"

"I just thought of something. I had an idea. A good idea."

"What kind of an idea, son?"

But David had no time to reply. He went into the barn, straight to the wall where the tools hung, and brought all of them out, laid them by the chopping block. The auger, the bucksaw, the froe, the mallet, and the drawknife. Then he sat down. He scratched his head. He took a long sliver of wood, drew a sketch in the dirt.

It wasn't quite what he wanted, so he erased it with his

foot, tried again. Several times he did the same thing. Gradually he worked it out. He saw what he wanted to do.

He stood up. There were some things he hadn't worked out yet, but maybe he could plan them later, when he came to them. Slowly he sat down again. No, he knew that was wrong. You had to plan better than that. You had to be sure.

He leaned over, stared at his drawing, thought about putting every piece together, about where he would find the wood for the poles and the flat boards, how he would arrange them, how he would fasten them. He saw where he had overlooked something, and he drew a few more lines, thought a moment, changed them a little.

Then he was sure he was ready to start. He reminded himself of something, though. If suddenly the whole scheme seemed useless, and he didn't think it would work, he would have to give himself time to think about it. To solve the problem. He had to remember that.

He began the work.

First he located a cedar bolt down in the woods, hammered the froe in the end, lifted the handle, splitting off one cedar board after another until there was a pile of them on the ground. He cut poles, straight, strong ones, and made sure they were the right size before he carried all the material back to his workshop in the dogtrot. He crouched down to stare at his sketch, to see which part he would have to do first, and what after that. He didn't some difficulty seeing the lines of the sketch, and he didn't realize why until he heard his mother speaking to him.

"David—I called you to supper three times. I spoke to you twice, besides. You've been so interested in what you're doing that you didn't answer. I guess you didn't even hear me. It's beginning to get dark, boy. Too dark to work. You come on inside for supper now, hear?"

For three days he worked. There were interruptions, of course, like having to stop to take care of Rosy, and carrying several kegs of water to the garden, and sitting down at the table to eat. Even while he was away from his job he was thinking about it, planning it in his head, wondering how to do this and that.

There were moments, too, when he made himself stop and think about something else. Moments when all of a sudden he wanted to pick up the ax and chop everything to pieces. He knew this would happen, and he was resolved not to give up. If everything did go wrong, it would be for some other reason; not because he lost his patience.

There were problems he had not thought about. Somehow, one by one, each problem was solved. A few times he had to take things apart again, do them over; he even had to remake the axle twice. But for some reason his mother didn't bother him with questions or put him to work on his lessons, and he was free to face his problems and work them out by himself.

A pile of shavings grew while he worked with the drawknife and made the boards and the shafts smooth. Shavings and whittlings and ends of poles and odd pieces piled up around the chopping block, and the noise of his saw and the hiss of the knife went on and on. Twice he had to go into the woods to search for another pole. Then there was the sound of the ax, and the rush of branches and leaves as a tree came down.

And at last, to the sound of his mallet on the wooden pegs, the strange contraption began to take shape. There was a great axle in the middle, there were thin poles running out like spokes of a wheel, and around the outer edge, at the end of each spoke, was a carefully shaped V made of two broad shakes.

When he was sure that it was strong and that the pins and pegs were firmly in place, he carried it down to the creek. It was taller than he was by a good two feet, and he had to hold it off the ground. He went back for more boards and poles, worked and hammered at them and moved rocks around, and dug a little channel between them so that the water flowed there, and then he carefully set his giant wheel down on the brackets he had made, letting the axle rest in the notches just so, making sure that it was deep enough for the water to flow against the blades—and he jumped back from it and held his breath.

Nothing happened. For just an instant he wavered, and his fists doubled up while he felt a sudden rage rising inside him. He caught himself.

There was only one thing that could be wrong now. There must be a rock that had tumbled in the trough and held the blades. He bent down, plunged his hand into the cold water. While the creek rose around his wrist, he groped for the rock. And found it. He lifted it out, and barely got out of the road in time—

For the wheel turned, the spokes moved, the boards flashed in the mottled sunlight, and a cup of water rolled off every V-blade as it passed over the top. He yelled. For the life of him, he couldn't help it. He yelled and clapped his hands together and bounced on the edge of the creek and watched the waterwheel turn around and around, steadily, without pausing, while each blade sent a dash of water into the air.

He ran back to the cabin, dancing and hopping all the

way. His mother was standing by the fence, shading her eyes and looking toward him.

"Was that you yelled, boy?"

"Yes, ma'am!"

"Something wrong?"

"No. Nothing's wrong. Now you just wait here at the cabin, and I'll call you when I'm finished. You just wait a little longer. I have a few troughs to put together. I'll let you know."

He ran back to the creek with an armload of cedar boards, the mallet and a pocketful of alder pegs. Then as many poles as he could carry. He pounded two poles into the ground by the water, crossed them like X's so there was a notch near the top, and set up another pair just the same way. He laid cedar boards in the notch, pegged them together tightly, and moved them out so that they caught most of the water that fell off the waterwheel.

The water flipped into the trough, ran the length of it, and out the other end. He went on with the work.

Within two hours he was finished. There was an odd, rickety line of wooden troughs going all the way from the waterwheel to the upper edge of the garden, and flowing all along it was water. Not much water, but a steady rivulet of it.

He put his hands on his hips and called.

"Mom! You come out here now and have a look!"

She came running out the door, past the end of the cabin, stopped, and lifted her hands in surprise.

"My land! What on earth have you done? Is that water running into the garden? How does it get there?"

He beckoned with his finger. "You have a look. You'll see."

They ran down to the waterwheel, and Mrs. Carder

103

gasped. The great wheel turned, squeaked, turned and groaned, and water ran into the trough and flowed downhill all the way to the garden.

She couldn't find words to say what was in her mind. Finally she shook her head. "David, I'll get some lard."

"What for?"

"Why, to grease the axle. Like they do on wagons. It won't squeak then, and it might even go faster." She turned and went back to the cabin, and he waited until she came back and daubed lard on the shaft. The noise

stopped instantly, and then all they could hear was the flap, flap, flap, of the blades and the steady swish of the water.

"David Carder," she said, "I never in all my days saw such a thing. I never imagined anybody could make a wheel to get water over to the garden. Land sakes." She glanced at him. "Something else I never saw, too."

"What's that, Mom?"

"I don't believe I ever really saw you before, young fellow. Something's happened to you. You've changed. You know what? You've grown up. Why, I don't even know if Jed could have done a thing like that, I just don't know if he could."

She tilted her head a little to one side. "Let's see now. How much water goes down that trough? And how many trips will it save you in one hour?"

David looked at her. "Mom, are you talking arithmetic again?"

She laughed. "I guess I can't help it. But I'm going to figure this out myself. Let's see—I can put a quart measure at the other end, and wait until it fills up, and empty it into the keg, and when the keg's full I'll know how many quarts that is, and how long it took. I can look at the clock."

When David went to the garden a little later, he found his mother sitting at the end of the trough patiently watching while the water filled her tin measure. The keg was beside her, more than half full.

"Mom, you're really doing it, aren't you?"

"Shh. Don't make me lose count." She quickly emptied the measure into the keg and put it in place again. "That's eleven. It was just two o'clock when I started. By our clock, at least."

While she waited and counted, David began digging more little trenches to carry water to the head of each row. He was scarcely finished when his mother spoke up.

"Sixteen. And it's full. Now I'll have a look at that clock."

She ran to the cabin, looked through the doorway at the clock on the mantel.

"Thirty minutes, exactly. Four gallons of water in half an hour. That's sixteen kegs full in eight hours. And it keeps on running, day and night."

David watched as the water ran down the rows, soaked

106

into the ground, but kept on coming. A little dam at one trench let it go down another. He followed along, watched the nose of the trickle as it moved.

"Now, David, you won't have to carry any more kegs to keep the garden watered."

"No."

"You'll have time for other things."

He stopped and looked at her. "You mean reading? Did I go and do something that means I'll have to work harder on reading and spelling and arithmetic?"

"No, Davy. Fishing. You've put it off long enough. Do you still want to go after those big fellows you were talking about?"

When he had tramped through the woods to the big fishing hole, he got down on his stomach and inched to the edge of the bank and peered over. It was just right. The pool was deep and the water moved slowly. The trees and the mossy banks overhung the stream. He could drop his line in the last bit of rapids and let the hook drift with the current down into the darker place. There was a big trout waiting there. He was sure of that.

He baited the hook, stuck the pole out slowly, cast the bait upstream a little, let it drift, down into the shadowy pool—

There was a sudden jerk, and a tug. He rolled back, watched the end of the pole switch around, felt the trembling of the line. There was an instant when the tug lessened. With one motion he swept the pole over and out, and the trout flashed through the air and onto the bank.

It was like that for the next hour, and when he had fished his way almost back to the waterwheel, his forked stick was heavy with fish.

He remembered to stop just in time. He had come to

the place where he could see the beaver dam, and maybe even the old beaver himself. "I'll see you one of these days," he whispered. "One of these times I'll sneak up and—"

He moved around a bush, lifted his head and stared at the shadowy pool.

Nothing happened. There was no sudden plop of a tail, no little waves spreading across the water. Through the trees he could see the flash of the blades of the water-wheel as it turned.

And then he saw the beaver. Sitting on top of the dam with its nose lifted, its head turned toward the water-wheel, watching it, was the sleek, black, fat, shiny beaver.

A grin spread over David's face. He stood motionless as long as he could. He suddenly shouted: "I caught you! I caught you napping! You didn't see me first, Mr. Beaver!"

With a sudden squeak the beaver bounced up in the air, whirled around and stared. He blinked. And then he flipped over, scrambled into the water with hardly time for a plop. Circles of waves spread across the pool, and

David laughed out loud. He had finally seen the beaver. It was a good feeling. It would be something to tell his father when he came back.

He crossed the creek on the stepping stones, went past the waterwheel and into the clearing, holding his catch of trout and his pole high, above the bushes. It was almost suppertime. The sun slanted through the trees, there was a sweet odor of pine, and it was good to be alive.

He stopped suddenly. He could see across the garden. He could see Betsy standing there, and another horse. And two figures, side by side under the dogtrot. One was his mother.

He began to run, pushing through the fringe of salal and galloping around the end of the fence. The tall man started running, too, and they came together with a great laugh. Two strong arms caught David around the middle, swept him into the air, pole and fish and all.

"Davy!"

He slid to the ground and stared into the kindly dark eyes of his father, saw the lean cheeks and the good smile.

"Davy, boy. I'm glad to be back. Mighty glad, son, to be with you two."

David felt something cold against his chin. He looked down. Jed howled with laughter as he looked, too. A trout, the big one he had pulled out of the creek first, was wedged between them. Jed took the forked stick from him and held it up so Mrs. Carder could see.

"Look at this! I believe the boy has lifted every last one of the fish out of Scat Creek. I don't think he's left a single one for me to catch."

They could have gone inside to talk, but there were too many things to say, and they stood by the cabin a long

time while the sun dipped low and the only sunshine was the golden light on the tops of the trees across the clearing.

Mrs. Carder wagged a finger. "Now we're going to have supper," she said. "We've got all the time in the world to talk, tonight, tomorrow, the days after that. I'm going in to get things ready," and she stepped inside.

David looked up. "Have we got time to look at the field? And the waterwheel?"

"We do, boy." He caught David under the arms, got ready to lift him. "Do you want to ride on my shoulders, the way you used to?" With a jump, David rose in the air, slipped onto Jed's shoulders. His father clamped his arms around David's legs, and David hung on.

Jed took a few steps. And stopped.

"Son."

"Yes?"

"It's not like it used to be."

"Sir?"

"I guess you'll have to get down. You've grown. You're heavy, mister. I don't reckon I'm about to tote you on my back."

Slowly David slipped down and stood on the ground. Jed looked at him. They both smiled. "Now, son, let's go see what there is. The field, and the waterwheel."

"Did you hear about Betsy? How I lost her?"

"I did. I also heard how you got her back. Now if you're going to show me something, we better hurry before supper is ready."

They went along the length of the water trough while David explained it all and Jed marveled and shook his head. And when they came to the wheel, Jed stared in amazement. Then they walked across the creek to the field and looked at that.

There was a call from the cabin. "That's your mother, Davy. Sounds to me like supper is ready. We better go back. Past the waterwheel. I want to have another look at it. I never saw such a machine. You're quite an engineer, son."

It was darker under the trees by the creek, but they crossed over and stood on the bank watching the wheel turn and splash. Jed sat down on his heels, snapped a twig and stuck it in the corner of his mouth.

"It's peaceful down here, son. I'd almost forgotten how nice it was. How about old beaver? Does he still have his dam down there?"

"Yes," said David. "And I saw him. Just before I got back to the cabin. I finally sneaked up on him and he didn't see me until I yelled. I thought I never would surprise him, but I did."

111

Jed looked at him. "You know, son, you and I are going to have to take a little time to get acquainted again. Something has happened to you these months I've been away. Something good. I can't say what it is exactly, except that you're not the boy you were. Maybe we can make a trip together one of these days. What would you say to that?"

David nodded. He was thinking about a trip he wanted to make. To Sam Skookum's village.

There was something else he was thinking about, but it was hard to put it into words. It was something you learned, bit by bit. It wasn't easy to say how it had come about, and just what it was. Maybe it was just something you felt. Or maybe it was all a matter of growing up. Slowly. A day at a time.